THE DEADLY
COTTON HEART

THE DEADLY COTTON HEART

RALPH DENNIS

BRASH
BOOKS

ISBN: 1941298133
ISBN-13: 978-1941298138

Published by
Brash Books, LLC
12120 State Line #253,
Leawood, Kansas 66209
www.brash-books.com

PUBLISHER'S NOTE

This book was originally published in 1976 and reflects the cultural and sexual attitudes, language, and politics of the period.

CHAPTER ONE

The man seated across from me wore khaki twill work clothes. They were tailored, if there were such a thing, made out of better cloth than the J.C. Penney ones and the fit was exact. I'd noticed right away that there were no salt stains under the arm yokes. If he worked at all, it was with his mind, and the clothing was part of a charade. His boots, when I'd watched him walk in, were highly polished and without a scuff.

Now he leaned across the table toward me and tossed back part of the shot of bourbon. He held it on his tongue until he'd absorbed most of the flavor. He swallowed and said, "I'm from out of town."

I nodded. I'd let him buy me a drink, but I hadn't touched it. That was part of my act. I was showing him that drink wasn't my real vice. It was supposed to convince him that I was a hard ass with business on my mind.

"They tell me you can *off* somebody for me."

I gave him a bleak look and said, "If the money is right."

It had started the day before. I'd been sitting on my back steps and looking at all the bud sores, the ones that would be leaves when spring finally made up its mind to drop everything and come running.

It was late afternoon and I was sipping a cup of hot coffee with a long pour of Calvados laced in it and Hump was in the bedroom talking nonsense to some trim who'd been warming his bed part of the winter. The part I'd heard led me to believe that the winter was over and he didn't need the warmth anymore. It was a kind of spring cleaning. I could hear her claws loosening and he was saying something about how he and his friend, Hardman, had some business to transact and he'd call her later if it got taken care of in time. Hump could lie with the best of them. As far as business went, we were about as busy as a dead cat down a storm drain.

The nonsense Hump was talking seemed private, so I'd taken my coffee and Calvados out back. I'd just been there long enough to warm the step when Art Maloney passed through the house. He stopped at the refrigerator long enough to grab the last beer. Now he stood on the top step and pulled the tab. He threw the tab as far as he could, almost to the stone wall that surrounds the terrace where I plant vegetables every spring or so.

"Litter at your own house," I said.

"Screw you," Art said. "A host is not supposed to talk to a guest like that. Read Emily Post sometimes."

"To hell with the old broad." I moved over and made room for him on the step next to me. "You come here to talk about my manners or drink my last beer?"

"The beer was an afterthought."

"What was the before-thought?"

Art and I had known each other since the time we'd been on the Atlanta police force. The difference was that he'd stayed on and I'd moved out. Just ahead of them asking me to. Now he was a good cop and I was off somewhere in the shadowland, making more money than he was but not asking a lot of questions about where the money came from.

"I need a favor from you," Art said.

"Tell me about it so that I can understand what I'm saying no to."

It took him time to get it all out. Between swigs from the beer can and a hesitation here and there, it went this way: an informer Art had a long rope on had passed word to him that there was a strange one moving around among the nightcrawlers. This guy was buying drinks and offering a finder's fee. What he wanted was a pro who'd do a killing for him. He kept his cards in tight and he wouldn't give out the name of the man he wanted wasted. That would be between him and the pro. The informer, seeing a chance to make a few points with Art, had strung the strange one along. There was a meet tonight. Either he had to furnish a pro or admit he couldn't find one.

"And the favor?" I'd waited him out and heard the line right above the bottom line.

"You might pass," Art said.

"Pass for what?"

"The pro."

"Not a fucking chance." I stood up and sloshed the dregs out of my cup. "You know the drill on this. You get some out-of-town cop and he comes in and parades around in expensive threads and acts tough."

Art nodded. He knew the drill. "The problem is that I don't have the time. I've got to set it up. I can't take the chance that he'll back off and take his business somewhere else. And he might just do that if I can't furnish him a name and a description tonight."

"Why me?"

"Two things," Art said.

Hump closed the back door behind him and stepped over us. He looked at the beer Art had propped on his knee. "So you're the beer snatcher?"

Art grinned and turned back to me. "You're available. That's one. The other bit is, even if you're made, if somebody knows who you are, that you're an ex-cop, it might still play because you've got a reputation like rancid salad oil."

Hump grinned at me, showing a lot of his own teeth. I got a bit of a burn and felt like telling him that if he'd been such a damned good pro defensive end, he'd have lost a few of those goddam sparklers.

"You sure this is a friend of yours?" Hump asked me.

"The *yes* just dropped fifty-two points."

Art looked at his watch. "I've got to know soon."

"Somebody waiting at a phone booth?"

He nodded. "Got ten minutes."

"Why should I do this shit job?"

Art didn't smile. I thought he might, but he fooled me. "Because you owe me one. At least one."

"Tell me about it."

"Runt and the murder squad. The time in the mountains."

Hump shook his head at me. It wasn't a *no*. It was more like sympathy for the fish that got caught. Hump said, "Must be something to drink in the house," and stepped over us and went back in the house. Along with Art, Hump's the only friend I've got. And there have been times when I've needed that big, black mean he carries around with him. For all that six-six or -seven and 270-or-so, he's also a sensitive stud and he knows when the talk reaches a point when he shouldn't be listening.

"One thing I hate," I said, "is a friend who keeps score."

That burned him a bit. The silence told me that. It hung out there like a frozen clothesline.

"Sorry," he said finally, "but it's down to the short hairs."

"Make your call," I said.

He sat there for another five or six minutes, not saying anything. He wanted to say that he was sorry but he couldn't, and finally he said, "Oh, shit!" and got up and went into the bedroom to make the call. I walked up the slope to the terrace. There was rot and the tree pruning that the winter had done. I'd have to clear it when I got the time. In my mind's eye, I could see those rows and rows of Chinese cabbage my girl, Marcy, had talked me into planting the year before. But we'd never figured out what to do with it. Hump had suggested that we bale it up and leave it as Care packages in front of Chinese restaurants at 3 A.M. some morning.

I was thinking about that and laughing to myself when I heard the backdoor slam and Art stood on the steps and waited for me to walk back down the slope toward him.

You'd have thought the whole thing was laid on by the C.I.A., by God. The meet was set up for the next night at the Blue House Bar out on Ponce de Leon. It was set for eight and I got there at seven. There was a van with a TV camera in it parked out on the street. There was also a receiver and a tape deck in there. Art and I went inside and picked out a table against the wall. Art sat down across from me and palmed a bug and attached it to the bottom of the table. We talked a bit and he went out and talked to the technician for a time. When he returned, he said they were reading it pretty well but that I wasn't to lean too far away from the table while I was getting the guy to spread it out for me. Before he left, Art cleared off the table and put a fresh ashtray on it, one without his filter tip butts in it, and said, "Good luck, Jim."

I looked over at the end of the bar. Hump was there. He'd offered to come along and back me in case it went bad. Now he was looking at me like he didn't know me, like I was just some white-ass he'd like to kick butt on and I was trying to get comfortable with the iron that Art has passed me as a prop. It was a Colt Commander, the fancy version of the old .45 automatic. It was bulky and I was having trouble keeping my coat closed over it. I'd left the clip in, but I'd shucked the rounds out and wadded them in a Kleenex so they wouldn't rattle around in my pocket. I had a slow beer and then a second one. I was looking at my empty glass when the man in the twill work clothes came in and stopped just inside the doorway. One look at me and I saw it register on his face. He'd matched me up against the description Art's informer had given him. Something like: 43 or so but looks older, balding, a bit on the pudgy side, wearing a tan suit.

It didn't take him long to make up his mind. He walked straight over and acted like he knew me. I went along with that, and I let him buy me a drink when the scuffy waitress finally found us.

He looked about my age, but he might have been a few years older. He'd kept himself up and his hair, a sort of reddish brown, was full and his teeth had been capped. His face had the long-jawed look that Republic Pictures used to like in their leading men back in the 1940's.

Without much small talk he got down to the business part of it.

I'd said, "If the money is right."

"What do you call right?"

"It's a sliding scale," I said. "A wino costs a hell of a lot less than a dude running for governor."

He shook his head. "It's neither of those. I guess you could say it's somewhere in the middle."

"Like what?"

"A business executive. Not a big company. He might make the front page the first day. After that, page 16."

"Fifteen thousand," I said, "and that's a special rate because of the recession."

He nodded. "It hurt your business, too."

"It's a joke," I said, but I didn't smile.

"The price, it's about what we expected."

I noticed the *we*. "Who's the guy?"

"Huh?"

"Who's going to be dogmeat?"

"Not yet," he said. "I've got to talk this over with somebody. I'll get back to you."

"I want a name." I made it rock hard, like it was standard.

"I've got my instructions. And anyway, how the hell do I know you're what you say you are?"

I let the table top cover me while I got the Colt Commander out. I held it under the table, not pointed at him because there wasn't any way he could tell if it was or it wasn't. That was a precaution. I'd seen enough holes shot in the sky while changing guards in the army, when you'd cleared the .45 and passed it to the next guy and he snapped it dry and blew a hole in some cloud formation.

I charged the Commander and looked across the table at him.

"Listen close," I said, "and name that sound."

The puzzled look on his face changed to fear when he heard the hammer fall, the dry snap. "What the ... ?"

"If we were playing cowboys and indians you'd be dead."

He leaned across the table and watched while I jammed the Commander into my waistband and closed my jacket over it. A twitch started just under his right eye. "You ... you could have ...."

"If I was doing it for real, you'd be gutshot."

"You must be some kind of fucking nut."

"No, all I want is a name." I lifted the drink. It was bourbon and my hand shook, but he was so bewildered that if he noticed he'd have thought it was his head shaking. "I didn't come here for a social. I came for business and you're not the only one who's deciding something. I get my say too, and to do that, I need a name."

"His name is Nathan Webster."

"What business?"

"Real estate. Bambridge and Associates." He gave me an address on Marietta Street. "That all you need?"

"I'll check him out." I waited a beat. "I'll need to know how to get in touch with you."

"Give me your number."

I shook my head. "Leave a message with the bartender here the next time you want to see me."

He nodded and stood up. "Check by tomorrow. I'll know by then."

"Right." I drank the rest of the bourbon and watched him walk out the door. As soon as he was out of sight Hump turned on his bar stool and started to move toward me. I shook my head at him and froze him in place.

Five minutes later, Art came in and said, "He's gone but we pinned a tail on him." He reached under the table and pulled off the bug. "It came in loud and clear, especially the dry firing."

Hump moved over from the bar and towered over us. "What now?"

"We find out who he is and who he's working for."

I stood up and stretched. "Another meet necessary?"

"Maybe," Art said. "We need the other name out of him. Who the other part of the *we* is."

"Then what?" Hump asked.

"Conspiracy to murder," Art said. "That's a no-no."

CHAPTER TWO

Marcy came by the house around ten. She'd been trying to reach me all evening. I didn't see any reason to worry her so I said Hump and I had been cruising around town, having a few drinks and looking at the springtime girls. The talk about the drinks seemed to concern her more than the mention of the springtime girls. That was the way we were. Our relationship was at that still, frozen point. Maybe if she'd been able to dredge up a few drops of jealousy it would have helped. No chance. She was that sure of me. The hard fact was that I was that sure of her too, though there'd been rumbles in the past about this man or that one. These phantom men made their appearances, it seemed, just about the time I'd turned down another position with some big security outfit, some 9-to-5 job with a fine future. The way Marcy talked about these phantoms, they were about half ambition and half great expectations. It was her way of telling me I didn't have much of either.

Still, the last time I'd counted, there'd been something on the fat side of twenty-five thousand in the shoebox in the back of my closet. In hundreds and fifties and twenties. That stack packed into a tight wad by the weight of the .38 Police Positive I kept there. It was unreported money, money that hadn't seen a bank in a long time and probably never would. I figured that was a year's supply, even with inflation. A year was a long time, and there was always the chance there'd be another shady job. Hump Evans and I were a pretty solid team. It would be the kind of job that no licensed P.I. would touch. Rank jobs that festered on the dark side of the moon.

The only two P.I.'s I knew in town had taken the safe way out. One worked almost exclusively for the insurance companies. He spent his time sniffing around ashes and finding torches under every bed and the rubble of every company fire. The other one carried a fancy briefcase and did most of his work in South America, security for U.S. companies down there. It was steady work with all that terrorism and the kidnapping.

Me? I'd never gone to the trouble of getting a license. I did favors. At least, I called them that every time I had a run-in with Art or one of the other cops. *Hey, I'm not doing P.I. work without a license. I'm doing a favor for a friend. No harm in that.*

Oh, yeah?

Marcy rattled the ice cubes in her glass. "How were the springtime girls, anyway?"

"It's too early to say. I'm not sure this was the first team."

"Oh, come on, don't hedge. Have an opinion."

"I think," I said, "that it is going to be a fine year for the rookies."

"Damn you, Jim." She got up and walked to the kitchen. The way she walked was like floating. I watched the hips and the shoulders. It was a body I knew pretty well, but I felt a twitch, an inner rumble, and I knew it sure as hell was spring. If all the birds and the animals suffered with it, I guess I could too.

Marcy returned with a fresh drink. She leaned a shoulder against the door frame and crossed her legs at the knees. The light from the kitchen picked up the gold highlights in her blonde hair, and I could feel the skin on that slim and fine-boned body under my hands and under my body in my bed. But the slate gray eyes were hooded in the shadows and I couldn't read anything in her face.

"I guess I ought to expect it," she said.

"Huh?"

"The way it gets every spring. You, Huckleberry Hardman, and your good friend, Nigger Jim Evans, all ready to build a raft and float off somewhere."

I grinned at her. "It passes, given time. But you'd better be careful who you call Nigger Jim. I'm not sure Hump's read the book."

A set of headlights brushed the front window. I put my drink down and went to the front door. I cut on the porch light and waited. Art Maloney walked into the light and up the front steps. I opened the door and waved him in. "A drink, Art?"

"A beer if you've got one."

I left them in the living room and got a Bud from the case I'd picked up on the way back from the Blue House. When I returned, he and Marcy were talking some about his wife, Edna, and the kids. Art and Edna were special friends of Marcy's. In the past they'd done their share of matchmaking with us. I felt that Art, a good Catholic, looked on the relationship Marcy and I had as a sinful one. I mean, it was all those pleasures without any of the responsibilities.

I handed Art the bottle of Bud. "You out cadging beers?"

Art got the message that I hadn't told Marcy about the acting job I'd done earlier in the evening. "I need a few words with you, Jim."

That blew it. I could see the interest and the curiosity on Marcy's face. I decided I might as well hang it all out and let Marcy sniff at it. "Go ahead. She'll find out soon enough anyway."

"I took it to the captain, the tapes, the video, all that."

"And ...?"

"I got a new lump kicked on my butt," he said.

"For which reason?"

"For using you."

I nodded. I could understand that. I did have a reputation that was on the far side of rank.

"He thinks we blew it. In a conspiracy trial we'd have to put you on the stand, and that would give some smart lawyer a field day on you."

"True enough."

"Even if the tapes were allowed in court, we'd need your half of it. And we need another meet. One where you dig out who this dude is running this errand for."

"The other part of the *we?*"

"I've made my guess," Art said. "And it's big, rotten big."

"How big?" I'd watched Marcy from the moment we'd begun to talk. She'd taken a chair across from me, put her chin in her hand, and she was staring at me with fixed eyes.

"The name Carter Williams mean anything to you?"

"Henry's boy?"

"That's the one."

Old Henry Williams had been a bit of a pirate in his time. He'd started with a dairy and a few wagons. By the time cars came along, by the time he'd had to move his dairy out beyond the city limits of Atlanta, Henry had shifted from milk and butter to real estate. He'd got a good jump on some of the slower developers. By 1965, the year old Henry died, he'd owned land worth on the other side of $100 million. After his death, it had been nasty. There'd been a squabble about the will. Henry's son, Carter, and his daughter, Eve, took it all away from their mother. It had a sour taste to it, the trial where they'd proved that Mrs. Williams was senile and unable to handle the estate. About two years later, Carter and his sister sold it all for a bit better than market value.

I'd seen pictures of him in the papers now and then. He was a heavy, brutish-looking man with a Neanderthal cast to his face. They always photographed him after he'd killed some animal or hooked some fish.

"What's the connection between Carter Williams and the guy I talked to at the Blue House?"

"You know the Williams Farm?"

I did. It wasn't really a farm. It was like some feudal estate. The gardens were famous and I always felt, without being able to prove it, that there were a few slaves hidden off in some remote corner of it.

"The one you talked to, Billy Ray Price, manages the farm for Carter Williams."

"Show me the connection between Carter Williams and the guy they wanted *offed*... the Webster man."

"I can't. That's tomorrow's work."

"It's all guessing games." I drained my glass and carried it into the kitchen. I added a couple of ice cubes and a touch of J&B. I took my time and gave Art a couple of minutes to sip his beer and decide how he was going to handle me.

He still hadn't decided when I sat down next to him on the sofa. It was time to push it back at him. "So how come you're knocking at my door this late at night?"

"Even though I've blown it, I need that other meet with Billy Ray Price. I've got to get the rest of the story."

"You say you can't take it to court with me as the main witness, so what's the drill now?"

"Purely preventative. We find out all we can and then we put it to Price. We scare the ass and the hide off him."

"Until he thinks better of it and goes back to farming?"

"That's it," Art said.

I sipped the J&B and scowled at him. "You've got a lot of balls, Art. I'm not good enough to carry this into court for you, but I'm good enough to shovel around in the shit for you. Why the hell should I? Give me a good reason."

"My ass is on the line with this one," he said.

"That's your problem." I didn't feel like talking about it. "Call me in the morning. I'll know something by then."

He left about half the beer. He found his own way out. After the door closed behind him, Marcy lifted her chin out of her hand and said, "You're rough tonight, Jim."

"It was that kind of a day."

"And sensitive, too."

"I thought you liked sensitive men."

Marcy shook her head. It wasn't a no, just an unwillingness to talk about it anymore.

She stayed the night. I guess the spring had slipped up and kissed her on the neck, too.

Art called late the next morning. I was seated at the kitchen table staring down at the packages of garden seeds Marcy had left spread out on the kitchen table. She'd gone while I was still asleep. Now the picture packages of summer squash, pole beans, radishes, corn and butter beans, all fanned out, looked like a nothing hand in a game of five card draw.

"We've got the connection," Art said. "Neighbors like to talk."

"It's too early in the morning for guessing."

"A wife, that's the tie-in. Nathan Webster's got a wife who works for Carter Williams."

I said I'd thought Williams was out of business.

"He is. This is something called the Henry R. Williams Foundation. It's a tax dodge of sorts. A lot of money sitting around and a grant every now and then. Nothing like the big foundations."

"It's paper thin," I said.

"Oh, hell, yes, but it's all we've got. And you know as well as I do it's usually the obvious one that nails it to the wall. People kill for love or money. Carter Williams must have half the money in Atlanta. That leaves love."

"You get a look at the lady yet? She might have a harelip."

"That's the morning business," Art said. He coughed. I knew he didn't have a cold. "Jim, you going to the Blue House and check on messages?"

I let him wait. For all the talk the night before about thinking it over, the spring and Marcy had fogged my mind. I'd just let it drift about in the back of my mind. "This one time," I said finally, "and now you owe me."

"When?"

"Six or so," I said.

"Call me and let me know what the arrangements are."

"If there is a note."

"Of course." He hung up. He was, I thought, about a breath away from a laugh.

I went back into the kitchen and warmed up my cup of instant. I leaned on the table and stared down at the seed packages. Even considering them made me think of all the work it would take to clear the terrace garden plot. All the blisters and the sore back. I tossed the packages in a kitchen drawer and went looking for Hump.

"Nobody can accuse you of being a fast learner," Hump said.

We had an early lunch at the 1776 on Luckie. On the way out the owner, Millie, reached out into the aisle and pinched my butt and asked where I'd been. I told her I'd been on the road doing time. The redhead waitress with the long legs stood at the bar counter and smiled like she knew it was a joke. Millie didn't seem that sure.

We spent the afternoon jumping from bar to bar. One drink here and a beer there. At five-thirty, I said it was time, and Hump drove me to the parking lot next to his apartment building. I got out next to my car and waited.

"You want me to tag along?"

"Now who's the slow learner?"

Hump grinned. "No red off my candy cane either way." But he waited for my answer.

I shook my head. "No reason for both of us to waste our time."

"Call me."

I said I would.

The day bartender at the Blue House thought he was a hard ass. Maybe he'd bounced a 97 pound drunk once. He said, "This is a bar. The closest post office is down on Highland."

I waited. I sipped the watered-down scotch. It was either that or he had the fastest melting ice cubes in town.

He weakened first. "What's the name?"

I took a long slow drink. It took me that long to remember the name I'd given Billy Ray Price. "Humphrey."

He reached behind the cash register and brought out a sealed envelope. He dropped it on top of the change from a ten. I decided there was a message in there somewhere. I put the envelope in my jacket pocket and pushed the five at him. He palmed it without even saying thank you.

While he was at the other end of the bar, I tore off the end of the envelope and tapped out the note. It was brief, typed.

Maybe we've got a deal. Meet me at the Regent's Motel, room 17, at 8 tonight.

I didn't reach Art until 7:45. I'd left a flock of messages all over town and I'd about given up on him when Sam Najjar, the bartender at George's Deli, answered the phone and waved a hand at me.

"You're a lot of help," I said.

"I didn't plan on another killing this afternoon." Art sounded short of breath, like he'd been climbing stairs.

"Anybody we know?"

"A small-time coke dealer."

I read him the note while I checked the time on my watch.

"You're going to be late," Art said. "I need to put a bug on you."

"How long?"

"It'll take me time to get it together. It might be quarter of nine before you can make the meet."

"No way."

"Huh?"

"He's already nervous. If I'm not there by five after eight he'll check out on us."

"You think so?"

"It's my best guess," I said.

"How do you want to play it, Jim?"

"I'm a ten minute drive away. I think I can make it by eight. Give me half an hour. If I'm not out by then you walk in and we lean on him from all directions."

"Without a warrant?"

"Hell," I said, "you knock on the door and I'll invite you in." I gave the watch another reading. "And I might even tell you some funny story about being offered a contract on somebody."

"All right." He let out a long hiss of breath. "Eight-thirty."

I'd made the first mistake the day before. The second one was knocking on the door to room 17. The third one, after a wait, was trying the knob, finding it unlocked, and walking in.

A billy or a blackjack came out of nowhere and landed across the bridge of my nose.

I went down in a lump. If they hit me a second time, I didn't feel it.

CHAPTER THREE

I opened my eyes, but I couldn't see anything. Something heavy pressed down on my face and I could feel water running into my ears until they filled and overflowed. I thought, *God, somebody is trying to drown me.* I swung both hands and hit nothing but air. I flopped over and found I was on all fours. I stared down at a sopping wet bath towel with an uneven red sunburst design. While I watched, a few drops of blood fell onto the towel and, following the fibers, diluted until the spots were a pale pink.

I shook my head and blood splattered in all directions. Out of the corner of my eye I saw the tips of a pair of black lowcut shoes. They shifted away when a few drops of blood landed on one of them.

"Don't bleed on my new shoes," Art said.

Somebody behind me caught me under the arms and pulled me to my feet. Someone else pushed a plastic form-fitting chair against the back of my legs. The knees buckled and I sat there and looked at Art. He looked fuzzy around the edges, but I could recognize the center, the eyes, the nose and the mouth that had Irish written all over them.

"That's some nose you've got there," Art said.

I lifted a hand and touched the bridge. The pain bounced off the back of my head like a handball. I heard water running in the bathroom and then footsteps and someone handed me another damp towel. It was a smaller one. It smelled clean so I bit into it and got some moisture running down my throat. The water tasted burnt and clean at the same time.

"Tell me about it, Jim."

I blinked at him. "About what?"

Art shifted in his chair and dipped his head in the direction of the main part of the motel room. My neck was stiff. I had to turn my whole body to look in that direction. All I could see was the polished boots and the legs and the knees in the tan twill trousers. The rest of him was blocked by the plastic-looking footboard of the bed.

"Who?"

"Billy Ray Price."

"How?"

"Take a look."

I started to shake my head and thought better of it. "Not unless you bring him over here."

Art pushed up from the chair and walked over to the bed. He looked down and then turned and stood in front of me. "Maybe I ought to say we *think* it's Price. He's got a head like chopped souse meat. Before it's packed in a loaf pan."

"Good country metaphor," I said. I was coming out of it and I could hear heavy breathing, like a dog in hot weather. It was a few seconds before I realized that it was my own breathing I heard. I was aspirating, my nose blocked, and I had a feeling that each eye was trying to look around an opposite side of a mountain. "First thing you know, you'll be talking like a real cracker."

I laughed. There was the sound like something tearing, the sound you hear when you bite into a piece of gristle, and I looked down and saw blood covering the front of my shirt. I choked and said, "God damn," and I started to fall forward. Someone caught me from behind, at the shoulders, and Art leaned forward and pushed at my chest. I said to hell with it and I was choking, spitting out blood, and the last thing I saw was Art's hands, bloody to the wrists.

I spent three days at Georgia Baptist.

The first day, they were messing with my nose and pouring blood into me as fast as it poured out. I lost a couple of units of blood the first night. It was twilight time and I kept moving in and out of the real world. I remember seeing Marcy a time or two, and one time Art leaned over the bed and said, "How you feeling?" and I told him where to stuff all that sympathy.

On the second day, I was awake when Hump walked in and lowered himself into the chair next to the hospital bed. He lifted his right arm and showed me a square of gauze taped to the big vein inside his elbow.

"You just missed out," he said. "Wrong blood type, or you'd be growing half moons on your fingernails."

"Lucky me."

"That was the choice. My blood or cop blood."

I blinked at him.

"Art sent over about half a duty shift."

"It must have been a direct order." The way they felt about me over there, it had to be.

"Didn't ask."

I looked at the window ledge. For the first time I realized there was a blue vase there full of tiger lilies. "You send those?"

"Me?" Hump hooted.

A pretty black nurse squeaked her way into the room and shook her head at Hump. "Don't excite him," she said.

"This honk? He ain't nothing to me." Hump eased his way out of the chair and looked down at her. "I'm just leaving. Maybe you could show me where the door is." He followed her out, hesitating just long enough to wave. Before the door closed behind them, I could hear him begin some candy nonsense. "Now look here, black beauty..."

"Edna sent the flowers," Art said. "They came out of the back yard."

I opened one eye and looked at him. "If they last another day or two you can ship them to the funeral."

"Quit whining. The doctor says you can go home tomorrow." Art placed a Samsonite briefcase on the bed. He was about to flip the locks when a nurse waddled in and looked at him. Art said, "Police business. I don't want to be interrupted."

The nurse said, "Yes, sir," and went away and closed the door behind her. For all I knew, she even put up a sign.

Art opened the briefcase and unpacked a portable tape recorder. When he had that set up, he reached into the briefcase again and brought out a large can of Bud. He popped the tab and tossed the tab in the briefcase. "Good for you as spinach."

"Thanks." I had a sip.

He handed me the mike. "Tell me about the other night."

Between gulps I laid it out for him. All of it, from the time I'd picked up the note at the Blue House until I'd walked into whatever it was that tore up my nose and ruined my good looks. When he saw that I was finished, he hit the *stop* button and put the recorder away. He stood around and waited until I tipped the can to get the last of it. He tossed the empty can into the briefcase and closed it. "Can't litter," he said.

I burped. "The cold beer was the best thing about this screw up mess."

"Bitch, bitch." But he wasn't smiling. I'd been breaking too many off in him.

After he left, I tried to sleep but couldn't. I stared up at the ceiling for a time and talked to myself. I was acting like a baby. It was time to put all that behind and get my crap together. As soon as I'd decided that, I found I could sleep after all.

Sunday afternoon. I sat in the shade and drank gin and tonic and watched Hump and Marcy clear the terrace garden plot. It was hot, thirsty work and every half hour or so Hump would come down the slope and pass me on the way to the refrigerator. He'd bring out a beer and stand in the shade next to me and toss it back in three or four swallows. Each time he looked at me he'd laugh.

It was my nose. It had a hook in it like the one the male dancer has in the Toulouse-Lautrec print. To make it worse, the scab crust was turning black.

I laughed back at him. He was the one sweating.

By dark the garden plot was cleared. Marcy had a sunburn and Hump had blisters. I rubbed vinegar on Marcy's sunburn. There wasn't much I could do for Hump's blisters.

I was up early Monday. I was reading the sports page when Art called. "Coming by to see you, Jim."

"You're up early."

"I'm bringing company," he said.

"Anybody I know?"

"Captain Wade."

That one. He was one who really loved me. Like he'd love a sister who whored for a living. I hadn't seen him in a long time, but I knew he hadn't changed. The last time I'd been near him was the day I turned in my resignation one step ahead of a review board. He'd stood in the doorway, without saying a word, while I cleared out my desk. From the way he stood, the burn on his face, I'd thought he was about to fast draw on me.

"Any special reason you're coming by?"

"I told him you were still sick. Otherwise he'd have pulled you in."

"That wasn't what I meant."

"I know what you meant," Art said. "Put on the coffee."

"I'll break the seal on a fresh jar."

I put on the water and got out three clean cups. I leaned in the doorway and looked up at the terrace. It was cloudy and gray, but the sun would burn that away.

Captain Earl Wade was a strange mixture of impossible elements. He was a straight, honest cop and he was also a politician. That was as difficult as juggling six iron balls in one hand. During my time on the force, he'd been the only one who could manage it. The others didn't have his balance. They ended up leaning too far one way or the other. Either so hard assed and honest they'd collar a crippled brother for littering, or so slick and careful they couldn't move without spending half a day looking at all the angles.

He'd grayed some around the temples and a few pounds had settled about his middle since the last time I'd seen him. He was about six feet, with a ruddy complexion and arms that seemed too short for the rest of his body.

"What was your put-in in this?" he asked me.

They were seated at the kitchen table. I was at the stove. "I owed Art a favor. He called me on it."

"That was some favor." Wade didn't look at Art, but the sourness was there.

"I wasn't eager," I said. I placed the sugar bowl and the milk carton in the center of the table. "Would you say I was eager, Art?"

Art said, "He kicked like a mule."

"At least one of you had some sense, but not enough."

I placed the cups of instant in front of them. Art added some milk and sugar. Wade drank his black. I doctored mine with a little sugar and stood with one hip braced against the kitchen counter. While I watched, Wade had a swallow or two. From his face I could see that he was cranking up for another bitch or two. I'd had about enough of it.

"There's one funny part about this, Wade," I said.

"Yeah?" He looked puzzled.

"I can understand why Art has to sit there and swallow this shit, but I don't work there anymore." I flashed my best take-it-or-leave-it smile at him. "You do remember that, don't you? That I'm not a cop anymore?"

"That's a funny attitude for you to take, Hardman." Wade had recovered and he had the slick oil pumping and spreading. "Especially after the mess you got us into."

"I didn't get you into anything. It wasn't my mess to start with and it still isn't."

"The body at the motel. ...." Wade looked at Art.

Art said, "Price."

"The murder of Price, it looks like you'd want to cooperate to get that straightened out."

"Cooperate is one thing," I said. "Having to eat a square yard of your crap is something else."

"I never liked you, Hardman."

"Come on now, Wade. You talk to me like that and I'm going to cry."

Wade stared at Art. His look had in it the you-should-have-prepared-me-for-this accusation. Maybe Art was ready to join the revolution. He shrugged. It was as close to the revolution as he could get.

Wade backed off and made a run at it from another direction. "No matter how I feel about you or you feel about me, you've been a cop in your time and you know what we're up against." It was the frat handshake approach. "You might not be on the force now, but you know the situation. With Price dead, without information who he was working for in this, the conspiracy to murder case blew up. No way it can go to court. All we can do is nail it to the wall so it can't go anywhere."

It was so convincing I found myself nodding.

"So, there's one more thing you can do for us."

"If it's something I feel like doing." There it was, right on the table like a big hunk of rotten meat.

❧ ❧ ❧

Art picked me up a few minutes after two in the afternoon. I'd been wrong about the weather. The sun hadn't burned the haze away. Dark clouds blew after us as we drove out Ponce de Leon. By the time we turned off into the roads that twisted this way and that, there was a light sprinkle on the windshield. We didn't have much trouble finding Fortune Road. You could almost locate it from the smell of the money. The houses back in there were in the two- and three-hundred-thousand range. And none of them appeared to be built on less than a ten acre plot of land.

Carter Williams' house, when we found it after a half-mile drive up a tree-lined road, was bastard Spanish. It was white stucco with a wide veranda on the ground level and, what might have been an afterthought, with a sort of widow's walk porch that ran the length of the second floor.

A light-skinned black in livery waited for us on the steps. As soon as Art pulled up in front, the black came around the front and opened the door on the driver's side.

"I'll park it for you, sir," the black said.

"Just a minute." Art took the keys and unlocked the trunk. I followed him and watched while he unloaded a tape recorder. He handed it to me and lifted out a portable video tape player and a small monitor. After he closed the trunk, he tossed the keys to the black.

"What is this?" I asked on the way up the steps.

"Show and tell time," Art said.

CHAPTER FOUR

The meeting was in the library. Shelves and shelves of books surrounded us. About half of the books had leather bindings. The others, most of them, still had their dust jackets on. All of them looked dusted and sad and unread. I had the feeling they'd been bought by the yard at some bookstore out in Buckhead.

Captain Wade had arrived some time before us. I supposed he'd planned it that way so he could get most of the groundwork talk out of the way. That was fine with me. I didn't want to watch any more of his performance than I had to.

Carter Williams, in white linen slacks and a white tennis shirt, sat on the leather sofa that faced the desk where Art set up his electronic equipment. Williams was tanned and looked hard as a rock. There was, it seemed to me, a perpetual look of confusion on his face, the look a dog might give when he doesn't quite understand a command. Watching him and listening to him, I decided that his body had kept growing while his mind had stopped when he was a teenager.

Seated on Carter's right was his lawyer. I hadn't caught his first name. The last name was Markman. He was a year or so over forty, but he dressed mod, like he was really twenty and about to set off for the beach where he'd meet a lot of college girls and get laid all he wanted to. His plaid pants probably came from Brooks Brothers and so, perhaps, did the red hopsack jacket. I hadn't seen his shoes. Still I could make my guess they were the white leather ones that all the lawyers and young executives wore on Peachtree during the spring and summer.

His dark hair didn't show any gray. He wore it in the Kennedy, carefully tousled manner. Under that, the round face appeared to be watching a poker hand being dealt. It was that patient and that bland.

I sipped my drink and sat in the background and watched. Art and Wade had passed up the drink offer. I'd taken one and I'd watched the show of displeasure on Captain Wade's face. Here I was, his big witness, and I was hitting the sauce. Not right, not proper, he'd thought. I was glad I'd taken the drink. It told me something about Carter Williams. I'd asked for scotch and rocks and I'd got what I'd ordered, but it was cheap bar scotch. It tasted more like shoe polish than J&B. Either there was a cheap side to Williams, or it said a few hundred words about the way he viewed us.

Art ran off the video tape first. It was what they'd shot from the panel truck parked out in front of the Blue House. It started with Billy Ray Price getting out of the big, shiny Chevrolet pickup truck. The camera panned with him and zoomed in on his face when he took a last look around before he entered the bar. Right after that, though it was after his meeting with me, the camera picked up Price as he walked back out. He stopped in the lighted entranceway. The shot was tight on his face and he was sweating. He remained there long enough to take out a Camel and light it. He had trouble touching the match to the cigarette. He'd been that shaken.

The camera panned with him to the truck. It zoomed back and waited while he backed the truck out and pulled away. It tilted down and moved in on the license plate. There was enough time for the tag numbers to be read through out loud a time or two before the truck moved out of frame.

Art hit the *Stop* button and the *Rewind* button.

Blocked by the bulk of Carter Williams at first, the lawyer, Markman, leaned forward and cleared his throat. "That's very interesting, captain." A thumbnail dug a narrow trench in his forehead. "Yes, I'd say that was really interesting." He didn't mean a word of it. It was green, lumpy, upper-class snot.

Carter Williams stretched. The muscles in his arms and shoulders roped and ridged. "That was Billy Ray all right," he said.

"If this is all you have ..." Markman said.

"It isn't," Wade said. He turned and dipped his head at Art.

The audio tape played. It didn't have the clarity of the old private eye radio shows I'd heard in the 1940's. The Blue House bar just wasn't a radio studio. There was no way you could control the noise levels. The scrape of a chair leg on the floor threw the gain needle on the far end of the dial. It had the thunder of a major automobile accident.

Most of the conversation between Billy Ray Price and me came out sharp and clear. For a time, I didn't recognize my own voice. It was southern, yes, but it appeared that a lot of the redneck had been washed out of it. You'd think I'd been taking speech lessons.

After I got over that amazement, I studied Carter Williams' reaction to the tape. He didn't show much. Not until near the end anyway. He flinched when he heard me dry fire the Colt Commander.

The tape ended. Williams, eyes closed, leaned back against the sofa. Markman took his time lighting a cigarette, composing himself it seemed to me, before he said, "That does change things."

"I thought it might," Captain Wade said.

"Carter." Markman touched Williams on the shoulder. "You know Price's voice."

"It's him," Carter Williams said. "I'm pretty sure."

Markman mashed out his cigarette and stood up. He moved around the coffee table. He was wearing the white shoes. "Even assuming that that was Billy Ray Price's voice, if we concede that, I don't quite understand why this involves Mr. Williams."

"Price worked for Mr. Williams," Wade said.

"We'll concede that as well," Markman said, "but that is about as far as we'll go." He walked over to the tape recorder and looked down at it. "I would hate to think that you believed that this strange conversation, this odd job search, was instigated on the behalf of Mr. Williams."

"Of course not," Captain Wade said. The hard line Markman took had Wade spreading the oil again. "That is the only connection we see. That Price worked for Mr. Williams. In the course of an investigation, we'll question anyone who might know why Price would want to hire a killer. Along this same line, if you knew Price well, we might even ask you the same question."

Markman nodded. It was the concession he wanted, not that it really mattered that much. It was game-playing time. You lie to me and I'll lie to you and after a time maybe we'll both begin to believe our own lies. And, with any luck, I might begin to believe yours.

"With that understood," Markman stared down at Carter Williams, "since this is informal, since no notes are being taken, I see no reason why you shouldn't answer his questions, Carter. With this proviso: if I don't like the question, I'll shake my head." Markman smiled at Wade. "That will mean he isn't to answer the question."

"Taking the Fifth?"

"This isn't a legally constituted court, Captain Wade."

"I realize that."

"But I will say that there is nothing wrong with the Fifth. It is the law of the land. It is not my fault or Mr. Williams' that the Fifth has a bad reputation in police circles."

Wade waited to see if the lecture was over. It was. He could ask his first question. "Was Billy Ray Price dealing on your behalf when he tried to contact a hit man?"

All of us watched Markman's face. Perhaps we should have watched Carter Williams instead. Markman nodded at Williams.

"That wasn't what I hired Billy Ray to do. He managed the farm for me and that was all. I swear I didn't send him out to hire a murder done."

"You don't have to swear to anything," Markman said. "You're not under oath."

I counted five beats before Carter Williams understood. He said, "Whatever you say, Bob."

Captain Wade got out a Kool and bit into the filter. He showed white, even teeth. "Do you know Nathan Webster?"

"Sure, I know him. I've met him a few times. You know, his wife, Ellen, works for me."

"Socially? Business?"

"Some of both," Carter Williams said. "I'm not in business now, but there are times when I need to deal with someone in real estate. Unless there's some reason why I shouldn't deal with Bambridge...that's the company Webster's with...I've been willing to throw some business his way now and then."

"Socially?"

"Well, they're both nice people. I invite them to a party sometimes or to dinner."

"Did Price know them?" Wade still hadn't lit the Kool. It wagged and dipped as he spoke.

"He must have. Billy Ray wasn't just an ordinary employee. He was more like a close friend to me. So, the people I knew he'd know."

"Can you think of any reason why Price would want Nathan Webster dead?"

"No. It's all so crazy. If I hadn't heard it on the tape, I don't think I'd believe it." He shifted on the sofa until he faced me. I thought I'd been forgotten. I'd been introduced and no one had mentioned me after that. Now I realized that his rather slow mind had been struggling with it. "You're the other voice on the tape?"

I said I was.

"And it was Billy Ray?"

"It was the man on the video tape, if that was Price."

I felt Markman staring at me. It was the look of someone with quite a bit of practice. He was judging me the way he would have in a court.

Wade felt it was time to explain. "Mr. Hardman is a former police officer we asked to help us. We needed someone who wasn't recognizable as departmental personnel."

The explanation had an undercurrent of disclaimer in it. Markman's cool smile said he'd read me and he could see why I wasn't police quality. I let the smile hang out in the wind for a time before I looked in his eyes and gave him my best E.S.P. *screw you*. His eyes flipped away. He'd got it, rank and with the thorns still on it. It didn't stop him. "What is your full name, Mr. Hardman?"

"Jim," I said.

"And what is your occupation now, Mr. Hardman?"

I didn't answer him. I lit a smoke and waited. Behind Markman Captain Wade, with a grim look on his face, said, "Didn't you say something about this not being a courtroom, Mr. Markman?"

"I think I deserve an answer." Markman wouldn't let it go. He wanted a kill. "If I were representing Mr. Price, instead of Carter, I might raise the question of entrapment."

"That dog won't hunt," I said. "And you damn well know it."

"Jim's right." Art fitted the cover over the tape recorder and slammed it shut. "You heard Price on the tape. Somebody might walk up to you on the street and offer to sell you a watch. Nobody walks up to you and offers to waste somebody for you."

"That's a rather simple explanation of entrapment," Markman said.

Wade cleared his throat and looked at his watch. "I think we've taken enough of your time, gentlemen. I have only one more question."

Wade was trying to shut it off. But the last look Markman gave me meant that he wasn't satisfied. His interest was up and it wouldn't take him long to get his answer if he knew anybody over at the department. They'd be only too happy to dump that sludge over me one more time.

"Is there any possibility that Price might have had some romantic interest in Ellen Webster?"

"That's hard to believe," Carter Williams said. "Billy Ray liked his women, that's for sure. But Ellen, that's hard to believe about her. She just isn't that type."

Markman said, "I guess that's all you want to know." It was final. There wasn't a question mark within a mile of it.

Captain Wade looked over his shoulder at Art. The electronic gear was packed and ready to be carted away. From where I sat, I could read Wade's message. It was in foot-high letters.

The hot Irish in Art wouldn't let him accept it. He didn't like the slammed door, the toe-crush put on the one question that hadn't been asked. He rode right past the STOP sign. "I've got a blank in here somewhere. What is your real relationship with Ellen Webster?"

Markman probably had expected that approach at the beginning. He'd relaxed when he saw that Captain Wade wasn't going to put a stick in that muddy water. Now he gave Art a hard stare before he whirled on Carter Williams. "Don't answer that."

"It's all right," Williams said. "I don't mind. I've got nothing to hide. It's just a business relationship. I suppose you could say we're friends. You don't work with somebody for a long time without liking them."

"You sleeping with her?"

"That question is an insult," Markman shouted. "You will not answer it."

Wade gestured toward Art. It was the cut-off sign. Art ignored it and said, "All it takes is a yes or a no."

Markman shook his head at Williams.

"A yes or a no?" Art insisted.

"Then a no." Williams was on his feet. For a moment it looked like all that brute power leaned toward Art.

Captain Wade stepped between them. "Now, let's calm down. You asked your question, Art, and you got your answer. That ends it."

"There was nothing wrong with the question," Art said.

"Or the answer." Captain Wade waved a hand toward the electronic equipment. "It's time we were going." After Art picked up the video player and the monitor, Wade guided him to the door. At the doorway Wade stopped and nodded, "Thank you, gentlemen, for your time."

I'd stayed off on the fringes. I was slow leaving. I put my glass on the table and picked up the tape recorder. When I turned toward the door, Markman was blocking it.

"You didn't answer my question, Hardman."

"Don't break your mouth asking it." I used a shoulder to push past him. He reached out and grabbed my free arm. I tried to jerk it free, but he held on.

"What's your occupation now, Mr. Hardman?"

I lifted the tape recorder and pointed it toward him. "How would you like this, case and all, stuffed up your ass?"

He dropped his hand and backed away.

I went outside and stood on the steps with Art and Captain Wade. It was an angry quiet out there. The young black brought Wade's car around first. Wade flipped the keys in his hand a few times while he watched the black walk away. "We'll have a word about this later, Art."

He drove away. We waited for Art's car.

"You hear those easy questions in there?"

I nodded. "Not a hard pitch in the whole lot."

Art hawked and spat a glob on the bottom step. That said it all.

CHAPTER FIVE

ater that same afternoon I made myself a gin and tonic and
went and sat on the back steps. It was sunny and cool at the
same time, that one poised moment before spring fell off the shelf.
Halfway down the glass, I walked around the side of the house
and inspected the fig tree outside the kitchen window. It had been
sick about a year before and I'd spent part of a morning cutting
away the rotten limbs. Like all surgery, it took time for the patient
to recover. Now, I thought it had. The tree was putting out pale,
delicate leaves and it didn't smell like cat piss anymore.

Back at the steps, I was congratulating myself on my first
successful major operation when I heard the car pull up in the
driveway. I waited. Hump poked his head around the side of the
house. "You didn't call," he said.

"Had nothing worth talking about." I waved the glass at
him and he nodded and went inside and mixed himself one. He
returned and sat on the step next to me.

"How are things with the top police undercover man and
superspy?"

"Crappy." He sipped the gin and tonic while I told him how
delicate Wade had been around big money.

"It figures," he said at the end of it.

"You or me," I said, "and they wouldn't have been tap danc-
ing around it."

"I can hear it now." Hump deepened his voice and put some
redneck in it. *"You been plugging that girl, Hump? Snigger, giggle."*

"No, sir, not me."

"You been getting enough of it? Hell, everybody knows you've been slicing and sawing away at it all year. Chortle, chortle."

"On my mother's grave …"

"There too? Snigger. Lord knows we're all men here and we know no matter how much it gets used it don't wear out."

"Not me, boss."

We were making so much noise we didn't hear the car pull up out front. And I didn't know we had an audience until I looked up with that stupid grin on my face and saw the man standing at the corner of the house.

Hump didn't see him. *"Would you say it is more like a peacoat sleeve or a rubber glove? Snigger."*

I turned and put an elbow in Hump's ribs. Hard.

Our visitor stood there, patient and indulgent. I put his age at thirty-five or six. Somewhere in there. His hair was straw-colored and cut close. None of that long hair for him. He wore an off-the-rack gray suit. It probably cost, at one of the late summer sales, about a hundred or so. His low-cut black shoes, dusty now from the walk up my driveway, had had a mirror shine earlier in the day. With all those impressions, I knew that his nails were probably neatly trimmed and cleaned. Like me, like all of us who'd grown up in the South, we'd had it drummed into our heads as children that the first thing a person noticed about us when they met us was whether we had shined shoes and clean fingernails.

I looked at my nails. I could have planted a garden under there. I guess you could say I'd outgrown that shit.

"You're Mr. Hardman?" His voice was soft and southern. It wasn't the usual mass southern accent. It was Charleston or Virginia, one of those places.

I nodded. His patience had changed to hesitation. I could feel him leaning toward me and leaning away at the same time. I was having trouble fixing him in my head. As far as I could remember, all the bills were paid. There was, of course, the possibility that he was I.R.S. From all that homeless money that passed through my hands, I only reported enough of it to appear on this side of poverty. And I'd had a visit once or twice.

"I'm Nathan Webster."

I stood up. Webster moved over a few steps and looked past me at Hump. I said, "This is my friend, Hump Evans."

"*The* Hump Evans?"

"As far as I know," Hump said.

"I've seen you play," Webster said. "It was several years ago."

"I'm retired."

That was enough of the Fan Night and Old Timers Game. "Unless you're lost and need my map or some directions, I assume you want to see me about something."

"I'm not lost." He continued to look at Hump. "I need to talk to you."

"If it's about the other night you can talk in front of Hump. He was backing me that night at the Blue House."

"It's about the other night."

"You want to talk inside?"

"It's pleasant out here," Webster said. "I hope I'm not interrupting anything."

"That?" I tried to laugh. "A routine we're working up for a Rotary Club smoker."

I left him nodding like he believed me. I went into the house and got a chair from the kitchen table. By the time I'd returned, Hump had asked if he wanted a drink. From the doorway I heard Webster settle for a glass of plain tonic water. I placed the chair for Webster and sat on the steps. A few seconds later, Hump brought out a tall glass of ice cubes and tonic. Hump sat down next to me and passed the glass to Webster.

"I don't know how to start this, Mr. Hardman."

"You can call me Jim." I waited. When he still couldn't get it out, I said, "Have the police talked to you yet?"

"Three or four days ago. They came to my office."

"And…?"

"It seemed like science fiction. I didn't believe it. Not then, anyway."

"And now … ?"

"I still don't believe it. But Ellen … my wife … she's been acting strange."

"Did the police talk to her?"

"They must have," Webster said. "Perhaps the same day they talked to me."

"You two talk about it?"

"I couldn't," Webster said. "It would have been like I was accusing her and I didn't want to do that."

That was the all-American marriage for you. Here it looked like the wife might be having an affair with her boss and the boss might have sent his odd jobs man off to find a killer who'd waste the husband, and they still couldn't talk about it.

"Something must have happened," I said.

"Two days ago, she moved out while I was at work."

"No explanation, no letter?"

He shook his head. "She didn't take much with her. As far as I can tell, she took only a couple of dresses and a suit."

"You tell the police?"

"No." He chewed for a moment on his lower lip. "I thought she'd be back, if for no other reason than to get the rest of her things."

"And you'd talk her into staying?"

He nodded. "Something like that. I guess it sounds silly."

It did, but I'd done my share of silly things in the past. It didn't seem fair to jump on his. "Have you tried to find her?"

"All day. I've been looking all day. None of our friends have seen her or heard from her."

"You said *our*. She have any girlfriends? Women she knew from work, ones she had lunch with or played tennis with?"

"Not that I know of," he said. "It's odd but I don't remember her ever being close to another woman, not really close."

Hump reached across me and hooked my pack of smokes from my shirt pocket. He lit one and placed the pack on the step between us. He was reading Nathan Webster, blowing the dust off every inflection. It might be worth the few minutes later to see how he saw the inside man.

"I understand this up to a point," I said.

The puzzled look settled upon his face. "I don't think I quite ..."

I'd gone too fast. I'd left him considering the fact that she didn't have any girlfriends and I'd jumped over some gaps, the questions that had been bothering me since he'd appeared at the back corner of my house. "Maybe it's not as simple as I thought it was. Look, why come to me? I'm the one who dumped this thing in your lap."

"Why, you saved my life."

That might be true, but I'd probably ruined his marriage. "What exactly do you want out of me, Webster?"

"You know Mark Hannah, don't you?"

I did. He'd been a good cop until one evening, off duty, he'd walked into the middle of a holdup at one of those 7-11 stores. He'd been carrying and he'd tried for it. What he got was a messed-up hip and a plastic hip joint that didn't meet departmental medical standards. The last I'd heard of him, he wasn't working.

"I know him," I said.

"He handles security at the Tyler building ... that's where we have our offices."

"I'd wondered what happened to him."

"Your name came up when the police talked to me. What you'd done. I knew Mark had been on the police once, and I asked him about you. He said you'd been honest once, but he'd been hearing rumors about you the last few years."

"People kiss and tell," I said.

"Mark said people hired you now and then."

"That's another one of those rumors," I said. "I don't have the state's approval for that kind of work."

"That doesn't matter to me."

"All right." I lifted my glass and got a noseful of ice. And a small sip of watered-down drink. "What do you want?"

"I want to hire you."

"Both of us?"

He looked at Hump. "He works with you?"

"He's the brains," I said. "I do the rough work."

He could smile. At least he tried to show us that he could. "I have a thousand dollars."

"That might buy both of us for a week." I turned a shoulder and put it between Webster and Hump. Hump knew what my question was. He nodded. That meant he wanted the job. I'd have to remember to ask him why later. Whether something in the situation interested him or because he was broke and bored. We'd taken some jobs for the wrong reasons now and then, and we'd been sick sorry later. "What do you want for your thousand dollars?"

"I want you to find Ellen."

I dipped my head. That might be possible.

"And I want you to find out what this is all about, why Price wanted me killed."

"That might be stretching the thousand dollars a bit thin," I said.

"If it takes longer, I'll get another thousand, two if I need it."

"You've got that kind of money?"

"My mother does," he said.

I stood up and dumped the ice cubes on the ground. "I'll need pictures of her."

"I have some."

"She have her own car?"

"Yes."

"I'll need the make, model, color and tag numbers."

"I don't have the tag numbers with me, but…"

"I'll drop by your place later."

"Seven o'clock?"

I nodded. I watched as he braced a checkbook on his knee and wrote a check for me. After he handed it over, I dropped it on the step at Hump's feet and walked around the house with Webster. I stopped next to the blue 1973 Capri.

"Two things," I said.

"Huh?"

"If I find your wife, I can't promise to bring her back to you. That's kidnapping."

"You find her, Mr. Hardman, and I'll do the rest."

"The second thing. I've got to pass on the word that she's left. The police'll have my hide if I don't."

"I don't like that."

"Look at it this way. The police can put a trace on a car a hell of a lot better than I can. And if they haven't written this off completely, they'll find out in a day or two anyway."

"All right then."

He was closing the car door when I said, "I'll need your address."

"It's on the check."

He drove away.

At the back steps Hump had mixed both of us a fresh drink. The check was on the steps. Webster had written it in some dark blue ink. The handwriting was oddly delicate and feminine.

I sipped at my drink. "Tell me about him, Hump."

"I have a feeling that his mother kept one of his balls."

"The southern mama bit?"

"The all mamas bit. What a lot of them try."

"But he's not fey?"

"Not yet," Hump said. "Maybe never. It might just be that thin-blood in the southern upper classes, but I'm not pissing at any urinals next to him."

"Why this job?"

"I want to see that woman. It's a fish hook in me. I think that woman probably saved him from Gay Liberation. I'd like to know why."

I found I was staring down at the check. Some freak thought had me thinking that the ink was going to disappear, just like in some WWII spy movie.

By the time I'd finished my drink the ink was still showing. For better or worse, we were hired.

CHAPTER SIX

Nathan Webster pointed me toward the hammered brass coffee table off to one side in the living room. About the time I slumped down on the sofa he switched on the overhead light. There were three color photographs lined up on the table top. I picked up the first of the photos. "This the whole lot?"

"That's all." He leaned across the coffee table. "I knew that Ellen didn't like to have her picture taken but, until I started looking through the envelopes, I didn't realize how few there are of her."

"You've been married how long?"

"Almost five years," he said.

"She give any reason for being camera-shy?"

"She joked about it. She said it was a woman's vanity and that she didn't want me to look back and see how much she'd aged since this photograph or that one had been taken."

"Possible," I said.

The woman in the photographs was in her late twenties, I guessed, and she wore her soft red hair shoulder length. She had the kind of skin that goes with red hair. It wouldn't tan well, and there was a butterfly sprinkling of freckles across her nose and cheeks. It was a long, delicate face with green, distrustful eyes. If you stopped this girl on the street and asked for the time, she'd know you had other things on your mind. That kind of look.

My guess was that all three photographs had been taken on the same day, maybe one right after the other. She wore the same green blouse in all three. In two of the photos, the waist shot and the full-length shot, I could see woods and a lake or a river in the background. In the full-length photo, she wore tight white shorts that had a defined crotch crease to them. There was a blur of a sailboat off in the distance.

"These recent?"

"Last summer," Webster said. "We were sailing at the lake with friends."

"I'll need one of these."

"Take all three if you like. I have the negatives."

I stacked the photos in front of me. The one on top was the head and shoulders shot. It was the one that would probably help most in the search. The shot of her in the white shorts, that one would give me a toothache. It was a body that had all the arrows built in. *Look here. Look there.* The legs were short for the rest of the frame, but slim and well-shaped. The breasts were a bit large and she carried them proudly, shoulders back and squared.

Just from the photograph I could feel the heat she gave off. If the pictures didn't lie, a bedroom with her in it would need more than an air conditioner. It would need a sprinkler system.

I opened my pad and uncapped a pen. "Height?"

"About five-six," he said.

I wrote that down. "She still wear her hair long?"

"Unless she's had it cut in the last couple of days."

I put down *hair* and a question mark. "Any chance for a drink or a beer?"

"I thought you wouldn't …" He seemed puzzled. "Not while you're working."

"That's regular police," I said, "and some of them don't hold with that either."

"I have some beer."

"Fine."

While he was out of the room, I had a good look around. It was probably a two-bedroom house and it was in a good section of Ansley. It wasn't the top money part, but still it was a hell of a jump from the slums. From what I could see in the living room, they'd spent a lot of time and money on the furnishings. Except for the sofa and the brass coffee table, all the furniture was antique or damned good imitations. Not that I knew that much about it. Marcy, if she'd been along, would have known.

The room had the smell of money to it and the patina of old family. It was a part of what I'd caught in the accent Nathan Webster carried around with him. What he hugged to himself like it was part of his heritage.

Webster brought me a Carta Blanca and a stein. I poured off half a glass. "You're not having one?"

He shook his head. "It's not my drink. Ellen liked it, this brand anyway. We were in Mexico City three years ago and she acquired a taste for it."

It figured. How the up-and-coming executive saw himself. There'd been that survey that said only losers and rednecks drank beer. The winners liked scotch. And only the best brands of that.

I had a swallow of the Carta Blanca. It was ice cold and had the strong flavor of the hops. "A couple of questions. You have any way of knowing how much cash she had with her when she left?"

"That was part of what I did today. I checked by the bank. There wasn't much in our joint checking, so she drew $800 out of savings the day she left." He paused. "I deposited enough to make your check good."

"Nice to know. She have charge cards?"

"The usual ones. BankAmericard, an Amoco oil card, Rich's and one or two more."

"That's one possibility." I wrote down the BankAmericard and the Amoco card. "If she uses them, we might be able to trace her. That usually takes a bit of time."

"I don't want to wait that long."

On to the next step. "Often when a wife leaves, she goes home to her family. You been in touch with them yet?"

"She didn't have any."

"None at all?"

"Her mother and father are dead and she was an only child. I suppose there might be uncles and aunts and such, but I didn't know any of them."

Another slammed door.

"She didn't talk much about her past," he said.

"Know where she was from? Where she was born?"

"I know that from the wedding license. Smythtown, Tennessee."

I had him spell it out for me. "Where's that?"

"I don't know."

He didn't seem to know much. A hell of a lot less than a man who'd lived with a woman for five years ought to. There were too many dark places. I'd always thought that a good marriage was one where each one held back about ten percent. The Websters appeared to be hiding about ninety percent of themselves.

"You meet her in Tennessee?"

"No. Here in Atlanta. She worked as a secretary at Bambridge. Later, after we were married, she took the job with the Foundation. Bambridge has a policy against husbands and wives working for the company at the same time."

"Any friends of hers come to the wedding?"

"Just people we both knew at the office," he said.

I put the three photos in my jacket pocket and stood up. I still had the open pad in my hand. "You said this afternoon your wife didn't have any girlfriends. That's hard to believe. At the Foundation there must have been someone she had lunch with now and then or a drink after work."

"There weren't any close ones, but there was a girl Ellen mentioned now and then. Karen Fisk."

I added that and closed my pad. "You said you have the information on her car."

He handed me a scrap of paper. It was a blue VW with the tag numbers YAG 341. I placed that in my pocket with the photos. I lifted the stein and had the last swallow. There was still half a bottle of Carta Blanca left. I picked it up and waved it at him. "I'll take this with me."

I drove the winding road to where it touched upon Peachtree a couple of blocks past Pershing Point. The beer bottle made a damp circle on my trouser knee. The sour taste in my mouth wasn't from the beer. It was the whole damned job. It didn't make much sense. I didn't need the cash and I didn't need the job. Odd how the need for some cash made a crappy job seem interesting. But this one, this one had me confused, lost, like I was driving through a thick fog.

Out there, God knows where, was a woman who seemed to have created herself as she went along. She didn't have a past and not much of a present. For all I knew, she didn't even exist at all. The only proof I had that she did was in my pocket. The three photographs taken about a year ago. It wasn't enough.

By morning, I'd thought better of it. I made a call to Nathan Webster at Bambridge and asked him to call Karen Fisk. A few minutes later, after I'd put on a suit and a tie, he called back to say that he'd talked to Karen Fisk and she'd be glad to have lunch with me. She'd meet me in the lobby of the Foundation building on Forsyth at noon. I was supposed to recognize her by her long blonde hair and her gray pants suit.

An hour or so later, Hump called as I was starting out the door. "We working today?"

I said I thought we might. I asked if he'd like to meet a blonde with long hair and a gray pants suit. The invitation had dinner and a drink in it.

"If you're paying."

"You short?"

"I could use a couple of hundred," he said.

I told him to meet us at Clarence Foster's. After he hung up, I went back to the bedroom, took down my shoebox, and added a couple of hundred to my roll.

The rear part of Clarence Foster's is a greenhouse. It's glassed in on all sides and there are potted plants around the tables and baskets of other hanging plants above. I keep expecting a leaf to fall in my soup. It hasn't happened yet.

Hump walked in from the bar with a drink a couple of minutes after we'd been seated. I waved at him and he arrived about the time our drinks did. A vodka martini for her and a gin and tonic for me. I introduced Hump to Karen as my associate and he sat down on her left. I'd taken a place directly across the table from her.

She was a tiny doll of a woman. I was having trouble figuring her age. I kept sliding back and forth between thirty and thirty-five. She had a lamp tan or she'd had a late winter vacation down south. She wasn't wearing a wedding ring, but she wore three other rings that had a lot of flash to them.

All the way out Peachtree Road, that long drive against the heavy noon traffic, she'd seemed pleasant enough. In the beginning I'd felt a bit of disappointment in her, that I hadn't been younger. I guess she'd adjusted to that and told herself it really was business and she'd get a couple of drinks and a decent lunch out of it.

I floated with it for a time. Karen and Hump made their small talk. It would have gone on all afternoon if I'd let it. I didn't. The object of the lunch was to find out something about Ellen Webster, not to get Hump laid. And it looked like it was going in that direction. I said, "I understand you're close to Ellen Webster."

"Me?" She laughed. "Nobody was close to her. And I'll tell you something else. Nobody at the office liked her."

"Nobody?"

"She acted like she didn't want friends. She could be distant, hard to reach."

The waiter handed out the lunch menus. I hid myself behind mine for a few seconds. All right. This one would answer the hard and nasty questions. She'd scratch dirt with the best of them. My problem would be to sift it. I'd have to decide how much of it was truth and how much of it was the distortion that grew out of the envy and dislike.

I decided on the London broil and closed the menu and put it aside. "Drink all right, Karen?"

"It's fine," she said.

"The story going around is that Ellen had a thing going with Carter Williams. You believe that?"

She nodded. "And so did the other people in the office."

"Any hard facts to back that?"

"They had lunch together once or twice a week."

I shook my head at her slowly. That meant I didn't feel that was strong proof.

"She was the only girl at the office he took to lunch."

"Still not enough," I said.

"You don't know her, do you?"

I said I didn't.

"But you know Nathan?"

"Yes."

"Well, Ellen is a certain kind of woman. She's got an itch that needs regular scratching. Do you think Nathan could scratch any woman's itch?"

I shrugged. That meant maybe yes, maybe no.

Karen felt that she'd won a point. She dipped her head and studied the menu. Watching her I could see that the lunch menu didn't interest her that much. By the time the waiter returned, she'd decided on some crab dish or other. I knew, without looking at the prices, that it was probably the most expensive item on the menu.

"And there were other strange things," Karen said after the waiter left.

"Such as?"

"She received letters at the office. Personal letters."

"Often?"

"Once or twice a week," Karen said.

"From town or out of town?"

"Out of town," she said. "One day the mail was placed on her desk while she was in the ladies. I just happened to pass her desk and saw the return address."

"And … ?"

"It was from some town in Tennessee."

"Could have been family," I said.

"You think so?" She leaned across the table toward me. "Let me tell you something. I've worked in a lot of offices in my time, and when you start getting phone calls at the office and personal mail there you can be sure there's more going on than meets the eye. Things you don't want your husband to know about."

"You remember the town on the return address?"

"No, I just had a quick glimpse out of the corner of my eye. It wasn't one of the big cities you hear about all the time like Nashville or Knoxville."

"It have a name on the return address?"

"Just a street and a town. No name."

"You remember the street?"

"It was something like River Road or Lake Road."

Before lunch arrived, she excused herself and Hump and I watched her walk into the bar part of the place where the rest rooms were. I drained my gin and tonic. "What do you think?"

"If anybody'd know what phone calls at the office and personal mail means it would be that girl."

"How do you figure her?"

"About a three-time loser," Hump said. He tapped the ring finger on his left hand. "You see that dinner ring?"

I had.

"Knew a girl once. Kept all her engagement rings. After her fourth marriage she had a ring made with the diamonds from all four rings. It would blind you."

I grinned at him. "Why only three for her?"

"I counted three big stones. Not as much dazzle to it."

"A tough woman?"

Hump shook his head. "That's smokescreen. Talk nice to her and she'll fuck like a goat."

I leaned away. "Then I'm done talking."

"I said *nice*. Not like a courtroom."

"Show me."

"Watch my number one jolly."

Karen returned. Hump helped her with her chair and grinned at her. "You been with the Williams Foundation long, Karen?"

"Three years, more or less."

"Ellen was already there when you came to work?"

"Yes."

"Those letters she got...she getting them the whole three years you knew her?"

"No."

"How long?"

"The last three weeks," Karen said.

"So," Hump said, "if something was going on, it had just started."

"I suppose so." Her mouth soured. It bothered her to have to correct the other impression. She'd wanted us to believe that Ellen Webster had a continual barrage of letters and a hell of a secret love life.

The waiter brought lunch. I backed away into myself and left the charm and the conversation to Karen and Hump. All the sparks flying around had blinded me, and I put my head down over my plate and listened. Hump must have passed *Indirect Conversation 21* in college. He'd veer away from Ellen

Webster and he'd talk about office politics. He'd talk about the godawful coffee in the snack rooms and then, as if by sleight of hand, he'd be talking about Ellen Webster once more. It took the central part of the lunch time and it didn't seem to accomplish that much. What Hump established was that Karen had never seen Ellen Webster with another man, that she'd never seen Ellen meet anyone after hours. All Karen knew was that, once or twice a week, Carter Williams took the girl to lunch and that the letters from Tennessee had been arriving the last two or three weeks.

Over coffee Hump gave her his soft, easy, wouldn't-it-be-nice-to-be-naked-in-my-bed look. "What bothers me is that, in these same terms, you've just lost your reputation too."

"Me?" Karen waited.

"Take us. Here we are out in the open, drinking, eating, laughing and talking. A sweet young thing like you and a fat old man and a handsome black dude like me. You know what some girl at your office might make of this? That right after lunch this old man and I were going to take you off somewhere and make a white meat sandwich out of you."

It backfired on Hump. Watching her I decided that it wasn't an idea with a lot of horror in it.

Hump turned and looked over his shoulder at me. The look asked me what he'd done wrong.

I dropped Karen in front of the Foundation building about one-forty or so. The drinks and the meal had mellowed her some. And I could hear the little wheels turning in her head. She had hopes for the big black nightmare that a lot of southern women had. I'd seen her pass Hump her phone number while I was settling the bill. I hadn't seen the look on Hump's face.

On the way home, I stopped by Peeples Liquor Store. It was a hole in the wall place. I wandered around the narrow aisles and picked out a couple of bottles of wine and a fifth of vodka. I waited while Fred Peeples argued price with a couple of winos over a pint of white port. After the door closed behind them, I let Fred total me up and paid the tab. He'd bagged the bottles and pushed them toward me before I took out Nathan Webster's check. He studied it and nodded and I put my signature on the back.

"You need any of it now?"

I shook my head. "How long?"

"An in-town bank. A week."

I said that was fine and left. So much for cash flow through my bank account. So much for the I.R.S. and their access to bank accounts. For the action, Fred would take $50. That was a hell of a lot less than the I.R.S. would.

It was close to three when I got home. Hump was waiting in the backyard. I unlocked the back door and waved at the refrigerator. I went into the bedroom and dialed Art Maloney's number.

Art's wife, Edna, answered on the first ring. Her voice was at a whisper. "He's sleeping, Jim. I don't want to wake him."

"It's not that important," I said. "Have him call me when he's up."

"About four?"

I told her that would be fine.

From the doorway I could see that Hump didn't have a beer yet. I opened two and carried them up the slope to the terrace wall. While we sipped the beer, I looked here and there to see if anything they'd planted had broken ground yet.

All I could find were a few blades of grass. Some spring garden.

❧ ❧ ❧

"You took your time telling me about it," Art said. He sounded hoarse and stuffed up when he'd called.

I waited out a long, hacking cough from him. "I thought you people were off it. Captain Wade said you were doing preventative medicine."

"Bull."

"You're welcome," I said, "and if I learn anything else, I won't hesitate to bring it straight to you."

"You got some interest in this, Jim?"

"Nathan Webster asked me to do him a favor," I said.

"That crap again? When're you going to get a new routine?"

"When this one wears out." I said. I got the piece of paper from the night table and read off the make and color of Ellen Webster's VW. I read him the tag numbers and he repeated them back to me.

"That's a lot of help. All she has to do is report it stolen or have an accident."

"She's got cash but she's also got an Amoco charge card."

"Might be too smart to use it," Art said.

"Why? She's not wanted for anything."

Art hissed a long breath at me. "I'll check. It's only been about three days or so. There's not much chance that any charges would have been sent in yet. Big stations send charges in about every other day. Small jobbers might do it once a week."

"Long shot," I said.

"What's next?"

I hesitated. I didn't know.

"That's what I thought." In the middle of another long, hacking cough Art hung up on me.

As soon as I put the receiver down the phone rang.

The woman at the other end of the line said, "Now I suppose you'll think I'm chasing you."

I didn't recognize the voice. "Huh?"

"This is Karen."

"Hey, Karen." I pumped in a bit of false enthusiasm.

"There's another one," she said.

"Another what?"

"Another letter. It was on Ellen's desk. I just noticed it."

"I'll be right over," I said.

"I'm not sure I can let you have it," she said. "In fact, I might be in trouble for taking it and putting it in my purse."

"I'm acting as Nathan Webster's agent," I said.

"Well..."

"I can have Webster call you."

"No." She waited. "Send your associate over."

"Hump?"

"Is that his name?"

I said he'd be right over. I went out to the back steps and told Hump the news. He put his head back and hooted.

"See what I said about goats?"

"It bother you?"

He shook his head. "It's been a long, black winter."

CHAPTER SEVEN

It was the usual dime store line of envelopes. The blurred postmark told me that it had been mailed in Smythtown, Tennessee, on May 27th.

Hump stood in the open front doorway. Over his shoulder I could see his Buick and the flash of blonde hair in the passenger seat. "You ask her in?"

"I think she was afraid of that white meat sandwich talk."

"An old man like me?"

"I said I'd take her for a drink or two."

I backed out of the doorway. The return address was printed in blue ballpoint. 2312 River Road.

I tore off the other end and shook out the single sheet of paper. It was bright orange. I unfolded it. The headline in large, bold-face type was *5TH ANNUAL SPRING BLUEGRASS FESTIVAL. THE SMYTHTOWN CITY SQUARE. MAY 30-31.* Under that, in smaller type, there was a long listing of the performers and the bands. I read about half of it before I decided I didn't know enough about bluegrass. I couldn't tell if it was a frontline festival or a backwater one.

Hump took the circular from me and looked at it. "This is all? Not even a word?"

Out at the road Karen gave the car horn a short push.

"The address is the right one," I said.

"You think there are any messages written on it in lemon juice or something like that?" Hump grinned. He wasn't serious.

"This is the message. We just don't know how to read it."

Another car honk. Hump moved toward the doorway. "Where'll you be?"

"Packing a few things. I've got an urge for some bluegrass."

"When?" He waved toward the Buick.

"It starts tomorrow night. Well leave about eight in the morning."

"Back soon." He went out and pulled the door closed behind him.

I reached Marcy at her apartment. The invitation to the bluegrass festival interested her, but she couldn't go. There was a big staff meeting the next morning and she couldn't miss it.

"See you in a few days then."

"The hell you say."

"What?"

"Get some steaks. I'll be there in an hour."

"Why?"

"I'll explain later."

Nothing surprised me. Nothing. By the time she arrived I'd made a trip to Cloudt's and picked up three steaks and some salad things. "Explanation?" I brought her a drink from the kitchen. The evening news was on, and she'd camped in front of the TV set.

"Later." She smiled. "Much later."

I settled down next to her. Walter Cronkite told us how the world was.

At eight I gave up on Hump. I got out the big cast iron skillet and placed it on the front burner. I dumped in half a stick of butter and pressed some freshly ground black pepper into two of the steaks. I'd just dropped the two steaks in and I'd turned to see how the salad was coming when Hump walked in. He slumped into the chair across the table from Marcy. He looked tired and out of breath.

I grinned at him. "Goats and monkeys, huh?"

"Don't ask. Please don't ask." He put a huge hand over his face and shook his head slowly.

"All right, I won't ask."

He dropped the hand. "But you ought to see her roommate."

Marcy finished the salad. I prepared the third steak, the one for Hump, and motioned Marcy toward the skillet. On the way by I passed the large fork to her.

Something bothered me. It nagged at me. I sat down on the bed and dialed Nathan Webster's home number. He answered on the third ring.

"Look," I said, "I think she's gone out of town. It's a feeling I've got. Maybe it's more than a feeling. I'm going to try a long shot and see if I can't trace her. I need to know her maiden name."

"It was Carver," he said.

A hunch. "Think back over the last few years. The end of May, this time of the year. Did your wife go out of town alone for any reason?"

"No." He hesitated. "Yes, three years ago. She said it was her high school reunion. Her fifth one."

"You didn't go with her?"

"I offered to, but ..."

"She was gone how long?"

"I think it was two or three days."

I thanked him and said I'd keep in touch.

We'd finished dinner and Marcy was making the coffee when Art called. "I've been doing your scut work."

"What's wrong with that? I've done yours."

"Don't remind me of that. Look, that Amoco charge card. The regional office is in Raleigh. I ruffled a lot of feathers up there. The kind of thing they'd do for the F.B.I. they didn't want to do for me, but I pushed."

"And ...?"

"They searched the new charges for me. They found a charge she made three days ago at a station just outside of Chattanooga. Gas and oil."

That tied it. It was more than a feeling now.

"Thanks, Art."

"That all I get? A cheap thank you?"

"I'll have more in a day or two." I looked up. Marcy brought me a cup of coffee. She placed it on the night table and sat on the bed next to me. "I'm going over into Tennessee in the morning. You didn't know I was a big bluegrass fan, did you?"

"You talking doubletalk?"

"You know any cops in Smythtown, Tennessee?"

"You've got to be kidding. I don't even know where Smythtown is."

"I'll get back to you." I broke the connection.

Hump leaned in the doorway. The steak had picked him up and put the fire energy back in him. "When you two park in the bedroom, I know it's time for me to leave."

I put an arm around Marcy. "Stay around. You might learn something new."

Marcy shoved me away. When I looked around, she'd buried her head in the pillow. Hump winked and backed away. A few seconds later, I heard the front door close behind him.

Midnight. A light spring rain tap-tapped on the bedroom window. Marcy lifted her head from the hollow of my shoulder and smiled at me. "Now you know."

"Know what?"

"Why I came here."

"No, I don't."

"You think I'm going to let you go off to Tennessee all randy?"

It made a woman's kind of sense. I just nodded at her.

It rained all night.

By late morning Hump and I were on the mountain road that circles high above Chattanooga. Below us smog and haze covered the city. It must have been hell on the eyes and the lungs down there.

By three in the afternoon, their time, we reached the outskirts of Smythtown.

It was a part of the fruit stand culture. Outdoor sheds and fruit stands lined the approach to the town.

"Question," Hump said. "What do you do on Saturday night in Smythtown when you're bored?"

"You beat your wife or you drive out the highway and buy yourself a watermelon."

"Or both," Hump said.

The town square was blocked off. All roads led in that direction. After a couple of attempts to get around the barriers, I parked and we walked the three blocks to the square. A large platform-bandstand had been constructed on the steps in front of the courthouse. A group of teenagers dressed the bandstand with red, white and blue crepe paper. Below them, in the street, another group unstacked and arranged a thousand or so chairs in a disorderly half circle. Wide streets ran down both sides of the courthouse. Down both these lanes, as far as I could see, there were craft booths and food tents. It looked like every civic group in town had gone into the business of selling cokes and hot dogs. From the funeral home names on the tent fringes, I decided they'd postponed all burials until after the weekend.

After some searching, and a five-mile drive away from town, we found a room at the Lakeside Motel. The battered old air conditioner huffed and fluttered and barely stirred the hot air. We had a view of a river or a lake below from the glass sliding door at the back of the room.

In the sun it was ninety degrees or better. Now I knew where they got their red necks.

At six, after a rest and a shower, we drove out River Road. The river curved with the road below us, to the left. The river looked muddy near the edges. Out toward the center, it seemed green and cool.

"You believe that crap?" Hump asked.

"I believe it."

"No booze or beer in the city limits. Dumb shit." Hump had found that out at the motel office while I was under the shower. "Should have brought a cooler with us."

"Bitch, bitch."

We passed a weathered shack with a sign about five feet high pushing out at the road. BEER. "On the way back," I said.

"Where ... ?"

"2312 River Road or a beer joint ... whichever comes first."

Another mile or so and the low, unpainted cinderblock building appeared on the right. It had *EATS* and BEER scrawled on the single front window. And in the bottom right pane, in a blocky child's printing, *THELMA'S.*

From the parking lot it looked like a full-up day. Cars and pickups lined three sides of the tavern. I pulled off the road and parked in the shade of a large oak. At the front door, I stopped and looked around. There was a number above the doorframe in chipping paint. I couldn't make it out.

Hump stepped around me. "Looks like 2310," he said.

"Then where the hell is ...?" I broke off and walked around the side of the tavern. Driving in I'd had the impression of a low building or a huddle of buildings behind the beer joint. Now I could see a shotgun arrangement of eight or ten rooms. Near the center there was a neon light, not burning yet, with *CASTEL MOTEL* on it.

I turned to Hump. "Want to bet?"

"Let's have a cold one first."

We returned to the front of Thelma's and I pushed the door open and stepped in. The smoke hit me and the air-conditioned staleness. Off to the left, a juke box was cranked up full and Mel Tillis whined "The Best Way I Know How," the song about the guy leaving all those empty bottles around his house and not even combing his hair. All because of lost love.

There were two tables available, one near the juke box and the other beside the side door. I headed for the one near the door. Redneck heads turned with me, tracking me. They didn't stay with me long. I heard the hum and buzz and the heads whipped away. They'd seen Hump and at the next table a beefy man in a clay-stained t-shirt said, "Look at the size on that nig."

An older man across the table from him shook his head, silencing him.

Hump slid back the chair across from me with the toe of his shoe and sat down. The only waitress was busy in another part of the joint. I got out a couple of bills and leaned on the counter. I ordered a couple of Buds. When I asked for glasses, the counterman flipped me two paper cups.

"It ain't the Midnight Sun," I said.

"What would the Midnight Sun be doing here?" Hump tipped back his head and poured down about half the beer in one swallow.

I sipped mine slowly and looked around. After the first startled reaction, the rednecks had gone back to the Friday business of getting drunk. I finished the Bud and pushed the empty toward Hump. "Get us two more."

"Your leg broke, Jim?"

"Going outside for a minute. Don't let these good old boys bother you."

"Why would they do that?"

I ducked out the side door. A sign near the back of the building pointed toward the restrooms. I didn't need the sign. A blindman could have found them by the smell alone. I went in that direction but passed them up and angled my way toward the motel office. The strip of driveway between the rear of the tavern and the motel was paved with broken beer bottles and flattened out beer cans.

I reached the door below the neon sign. A card in the window part of the door had *OFFICE* written on it. I pushed the door open and went in. There was a counter off to the right. Straight ahead there was an open door and beyond that an unmade bed. I leaned on the counter and waited. Near my elbow I saw a thick stack of the flyers for the festival, identical to the one that had been mailed to Ellen Webster.

I waited. A couple of minutes passed and then I heard a toilet flush. The sound came from the direction of the bedroom. Another minute or so and a woman appeared in the doorway. She wore jean pants and boots and a white cotton top. Huge breasts sagged. No bra. She looked about forty and her hair was bleached. Either her eyebrows had been touched up or they'd grown back in coal black.

"We don't have any rooms," she said from the doorway. "Full up."

"It's not that."

"What is it then?" Keeping her distance, she rounded the counter and placed it between us.

"I'm here for the bluegrass festival."

She waited. Her face showed nothing.

"I thought a friend of mine might be registered here."

"Who's that?"

"Ellen Carver."

"She's not."

"Well," I said, "maybe I misunderstood her."

Flat eyes, unblinking. "That all you want?"

"You know Ellen Carver? She's from around here."

"There must be ten thousand people live here in town. You know ten thousand people?"

"You've got me there." I nodded my thanks and backed toward the door.

She leaned across the counter top. "You want to leave your name in case she comes in?"

I said, "No reason to do that. You're full up, right?"

The heat and humidity hit me with the force of a two-by-four. I took a deep breath and stepped out into the driveway. I looked down the row of cars parked in front of the motel rooms. I didn't see a blue VW. Before I headed back to Thelma's, I looked toward the motel office. The woman had her face pressed to the pane above the office sign. I waved at her.

The stale air conditioning felt better now. I eased into the chair across the table from Hump. There were two empties in front of him. "Where's mine?"

"I drank it." Hump leaned toward me. "The vibrations in here are bad, bad, bad."

"And it's driving you to drink?" I looked around the room. About forty pairs of eyes burned at me. "Anything happen?"

He shook his head. "I think some of these cowboys never saw a black before."

"Let them choke on the experience." I got the empties and carried them to the bar counter. When the counterman approached, I nodded at the bottles. Reluctantly, I thought, he opened two more.

"No trouble in here," the counterman said under his breath when he gave me my change.

"Why should there be trouble?"

"It's the nig ... your friend."

"I'll tell him you're concerned about him." I turned away.

"No, wait …"

I pushed a beer toward Hump. "You been making trouble in here? Playing grab ass with their ladies?"

"What ladies?"

He was right. The only woman besides the waitress in the room was fat and almost toothless. "Screw them."

I got out a handful of change and marched to the juke box. I didn't see any songs I liked so I played "Jingle Bell Rock" three times.

The two uniformed Smythtown cops came in the bar exactly at seven-thirty. I'd just checked the time by the Schlitz clock over the menu board. One slow look around the room and they headed straight for our table. I should have expected it. It was that kind of town. It looked like we were going to be arrested to prevent a race riot.

Both of them were pretty young, not much more than twenty. The one who stepped out first and led the way to our table was still fighting acne. There was a bad patch of it across his chin. He stopped at the end of our table. The other one drifted away so that he was behind Hump, facing me.

"You two visiting town?"

"We're here for the bluegrass," I said.

"Where from?"

"Atlanta."

"A long way to come just for music," the cop behind Hump said.

"Not if you're a real fan," I said.

"You two traveling together?" This from the one with the acne patch on his chin. He'd taken over again.

I nodded. "You got some good reason for asking these questions?"

"We've got reason," he said.

"Give us one," I said.

"Word is somebody is selling dope over at the festival." He dipped his head at me. "You fit the description."

"Where'd you get the description?"

"A phone call," he said.

"They give you their name?"

He shook his head. "We've got a Dope Hotline here. People don't have to give their names to report a crime."

"Easy on them," I said. "What now?"

"We go down to the station and you talk to the chief."

"You mean you're not the chief?"

Hump laughed.

"Act any way you want to with me," the young cop said, "but you'll watch your mouth with Turk Edwards. He don't take shit off anybody." The way he said it had pride and awe all tied up together.

The name rang a bell somewhere. I couldn't place it. Across the table from me, Hump smiled and lowered an eyelid at me. I don't know what he meant.

"Let's go talk to the chief," Hump said. He was still smiling when he tipped back his bottle and drained it.

CHAPTER EIGHT

The police station had the minimum furniture. Two desks behind a waist-high counter. The walls were bathroom green and there was the fresh smell of the paint. It was spring cleaning or some sprucing up for the festival.

Hump and I got edged in until we faced the counter. The quiet young cop stood gun on us, the heel of his right hand lightly on the top of the butt of his holstered gun. The other one danced around the end of the counter. "Chief, we've got them."

No answer. I could hear water running past the partly open door straight ahead.

Acne chin took in a deep breath and yelled, "Chief!"

The water stopped. The man who came through the door was probably forty or forty-one. He was five-eleven or so, broad in the shoulders and a little bowlegged. His tanned face had sun squint wrinkles in it. He wore the tan uniform pants and a short sleeve white shirt with his badge pinned on it.

"What you yelling about, Ed?"

"We picked up these two at Thelma's."

"The drug tip?" The chief hadn't looked at us. He was drying his face with three or four paper towels.

"Dead right."

I smiled to myself. I guess that was the way he thought cops talked. I looked over my right shoulder at Hump. He had about the biggest bird-eating grin I'd ever seen on anybody's face.

"You search the car yet, Ed?"

"Not yet, Chief."

"Get to it then." The chief turned and dropped the wad of paper towels in a trash can beside the office door.

"It's still ..." Ed mumbled.

"What?"

"It's still out at Thelma's."

"Go get it, you dumbass. What kind of police work ... ?" The chief lifted his head and looked at us for the first time. Maybe not looking at us was part of his act, letting us know that we didn't matter one bit to him. One look at Hump and I saw his mouth drop open a couple of inches, and I saw the amazement and the recognition.

"Hump, you son of a bitch, is that you?"

"In the black flesh," Hump said. "If I'd known you were chief here, Turk, I'd have got arrested sooner."

The chief started past the young cop. His hand was out. The young cop couldn't take the surprise. He said, "You know this nig, Turk?"

It was so fast I'm not even sure I saw the blur of Turk's hand. He hit the young cop with an open hand. It sounded like a closeup thunderclap. Ed's head flew back and his cap skidded across the floor and didn't stop until it reached the wall.

Turk grabbed him by the shirt front. "Ed, I don't know if you're going to make it in police work, boy."

"But ..."

"You're going to be working in Allgood's garage again next week if you don't grow some manners. You know who you just arrested?"

"The tip said ..."

"You arrested my friend, Hump. Why, we played ball together at Cleveland."

"The tip we got ..."

Turk shoved him away. "You selling dope now, Hump?"

"Came to hear the music," Hump said. "I'm not selling anything on this trip."

"Your friend there?"

"He's clean."

"You hear that?" Turk yelled at the two young cops. "If you heard that, then you get your asses out there and arrest me some real dope dealers."

The two cops sprinted for the outside door. Turk watched them go. He walked over and picked up Ed's cap. "Help ain't what it used to be."

"I read that somewhere," Hump said.

Turk dropped the cap on the nearest desk and they shook hands. As soon as Hump got his hand free, he waved it at me. Turk repeated my name to himself a couple of times so he'd remember it. I could see his lips move.

It was coming back to me. Turk Edwards did mean something to me, after all. He'd been a hell of a free safety in his time. He'd played for two or three teams, but he'd finished up at Cleveland.

"How do you like our town?" Turk asked.

"A lot of charm," I said.

"You know there's no drinking here in town?"

"That's why we were out at Thelma's," Hump said.

"Come on back to my office." Turk led the way. There was a new metal cooler on the battered desk. Turk flipped open the top and pulled out three Stroh's. "Confiscated this off some long hairs over at the square. Those boys were dumb careless." He closed the top and ran his hand over the finish. "I've got a feeling this is going to come in handy on fishing trips this spring."

I found myself a seat and settled down with the Stroh's. It was old home week and I sat off at the edges of it and listened to them run through the when-is-the-last-time-you-saw routines. It was ten minutes by the clock over the desk before they ran out of names. I had a feeling it might have lasted longer, but neither Turk nor Hump seemed to have kept up with their old teammates.

Turk dropped his empty in a trash can behind the desk. While he popped the top on another he said, "I see you're still hanging around the wrong kinds of places, Hump."

"Smelled the beer," Hump said.

"That all you smelled out there?"

The grin just this side of a leer told me all I needed to know. "The motel?"

"If you want to call it that." Turk laughed. "Well, these farm boys have to learn about women somewhere. At that, it's still nothing like Atlanta. The last thing I heard there must be two or three thousand of those lost women walking up and down Peachtree."

"My girl won't let me do a head count," I said.

Turk looked at me with some new interest. "You made the place right away, huh?"

"Jim used to be with the Atlanta police," Hump said.

"That right? What tipped you?"

"I met the manager."

"Emma? A bottle blonde with a shape like a trash bag?"

I nodded.

"Manager is a kind way to talk about her."

"The town winks at it?"

"The chief before me … Handy Spence … he said he thought it kept rapes down. And it gave work to girls too lazy to work in the dime store or the supermarket."

"Ahead of his time," I said. I dropped an empty and got myself another Stroh's. "You've been chief how long?"

"A bit more than three years."

"Then you didn't know Ellen Carver?" It wasn't the right way to throw that in. Maybe there wasn't a right way.

Turk placed his beer bottle on the desk and pushed back his chair. He went into the bathroom and wet a couple of paper towels. When he returned to the office, he was wiping his face and arms.

"Next year I'm going to be air-conditioned if I have to send those two idiots down to the Morse Appliance Store and break and enter." He wadded the paper towels and tossed them in the trash can. He hooked his thumbs in his belt and tipped his head toward Hump. "You sure this is a friend of yours?"

"He's straight with me," Hump said.

"He's about to get crooked with me," Turk said.

"I'd be sorry about that."

"You ought to be." He jerked his right thumb from his belt. He lifted his Stroh's. The look on his face said that it didn't taste right anymore. "Jim Hardman, that right?"

"That's my name."

"Show me your license," Turk said.

"A P.I. license? I don't have one."

Turk turned and walked to the window. He stood there for a long time. It was so still I could hear the string instruments from the bands playing on the square. "You're missing some good bluegrass tonight."

I waited.

"But you didn't come for that, did you?"

"I could stand a couple of hours of it," I said.

He whirled and moved to the desk. "Every time I think this thing is buried, another one of your kind starts trying to dig it up again."

"I'm not following you."

"The hell you're not. Let me tell you something. Nobody blows smoke up my ass. Nobody." He waved his beer at Hump. "You tell him."

"Not in the old days," Hump said.

"And not today either," Turk said. "You traced it this far. That's one step past anybody else. You must be good at it."

"I put in my time," I said. The fog was blowing in. It didn't make one bit of sense. He talked like I knew something that I didn't, and I knew if I admitted that, I'd never find out what it was. The well would dry up damned fast. Or, as they used to say in con circles, the pump handle would pull out. "Tell me about her, Chief."

"Not on your fat ass, Charley."

"Then I'll tell you what I know. I think she's in town."

"She wouldn't come back here. She knows better."

"It's a good time for it," I said. "You've got forty or fifty thousand strangers in town for the festival. What's one more strange face?"

"Slow it down," Hump said. "This is flying past me too fast."

"You expect me to believe that?"

"It's the truth."

"You've been in town how long?"

"Since this afternoon," Hump said.

"And right away you're camped out in front of the motel? Don't try to shit me, Hump."

Slow, slow, all those brain cells dying every year. It took me longer than it should have. "She worked there?"

"Seven or eight years ago. She was still in her teens. Eighteen or so."

"Ellen Carver was hooking?"

"It wasn't Carver then. That was later. It was Abse then."

"A local girl?"

"From outside of town, between here and Corkville."

"Ellen Abse." I tried out the name.

"It was Cora Abse when she worked the flatback trade," Turk said.

"And what happened?"

Turk laughed. Spit flew across the desk. "You tell this buddy of yours, Hump, that I've spent time in the city. This dumb act won't get him a nickel's worth of anything from me."

I spread my hands in a gesture of apology. "I had to try it."

"And you got what it was worth."

"Seems so."

He was running in circles too. He came back and faced it finally. "You say you think she's in town?"

"I had a feeling she was headed this way."

"Just a feeling?"

"More than that."

"You said you talked to Emma at the motel?"

I nodded.

"You asked about Ellen Carver?"

"I asked."

"That explains the call to the Dope Hotline." He grinned at me. "This the way you people do police work in Atlanta?"

"When we don't know enough to do it any other way."

"Funny thing." He said it slow, musing. There was a coat rack in the back corner of the office. He got his uniform jacket and hooked a finger in the neck and slung it over his shoulder. "You asked Emma about Ellen Carver. She puts my boys on you. Wonder why she's freaking out like that. It's not like her."

I stood up and tossed back the last of my Stroh's.

"You boys enjoy the festival." Turk reached the doorway.

"Wait a minute."

He turned and put a hand on the door frame. "Yeah?"

"My car's out at Thelma's."

"And you want a ride?"

"Your boys brought us in. It just seems fair."

After a long hesitation, he nodded. He drove us out the river road to Thelma's. He didn't say a word the whole time.

Turk stopped the police car in front of Thelma's. Hump slid out and held the door open for me. I moved in that direction before Turk touched my arm and turned me back toward him. "You two owe me a beer. I'll be in to collect it in a minute or two."

"After you talk to Emma?"

"Yeah."

I stepped out. "Glad to buy you the beer."

"And you owe me some truth."

"That might be harder to get." I closed the door.

He threw rocks and dust going around the side of the beer joint. At the front door, I thought better of it and told Hump to go in and order us a beer. I headed for the motel at a fast walk. I reached it just as the door to the office closed behind him. I edged over to the window part of the door and looked in. He was leaning with his arms straight on the counter. Emma, dressed in a pink terrycloth robe, was behind the counter. Turk said something I didn't hear. She shook her head. He repeated it. She shook her head once more. His right hand moved about four inches. It hit her flush on the side of the jaw. She fell back, out of sight behind the counter. He pressed his stomach against the counter and leaned over it. He said something. It was about half a minute before she pulled herself up. She braced herself against the counter. She was shaking her head, like she was trying to get the cobwebs out of it.

He asked his question again. This time she answered him. It was one of those times when I wished I could read lips.

I turned away and headed for the beer bar. I was about halfway there when I heard him coming up behind me. He moved pretty fast.

"Hear enough, Hardman?"

"I didn't hear anything."

He caught my elbow and turned me. "You boys from the big city have bad habits."

"That might be, but I gave up slapping women years go."

"She was wasting my time. She wanted me to stand around asking that question all night."

"And you got your answer?"

"I got it," he said. He released my arm and moved up level with me. "Now I'm ready for that beer you owe me."

"I was right?"

"She was here. Stayed one night and left this morning."

"Going where?"

"Emma didn't know."

"Why was she here?"

"Emma didn't know that either."

We reached the side door. "Emma doesn't seem to know very much."

"It was the truth," Turk said.

"You sure?"

He nodded. "She was scared enough to tell me."

"Unless she's more afraid of somebody else."

Over beers in Thelma's, I asked when Emma had said Ellen Carver had left.

"Eight-thirty or nine this morning. Is that important?"

"I don't know."

"You sure do have a talent for walking around a question." Turk narrowed his eyes and faced Hump. "You used to talk straight back some years ago."

Hump shook his head. "I've had special training since then."

"In lying?"

"In close-mouth."

"It's the same thing." He turned on me. "I'd like to know who you're working for."

"Ourselves. I like girls."

"Some years back I might have believed you. Words I hear lead me to believe Cora was the best in the state at a couple of those bedroom games and that's from some people who have made a statewide study of it." Turk waved his empty at the counterman who sprinted over to the table with three more Buds. "You're from Atlanta so I'm going to guess that you're working for somebody there. And that thought confuses me. As far as I know, nobody involved with this royal fuckup lives in Atlanta. And that makes me believe that this animal has grown a few more legs."

"I'll tell you who I'm working for if you'll tell me what it's about."

"You never stop trying." He shook his head.

"It's a fair deal." I reached into my coat pocket and tore out a couple of deposit slips from the back of my checkbook. I placed one slip in front of Turk and kept one for myself. "This is the deal. I'll write down my interest in the girl and you write down what the big secret is."

"This some trick?"

"No."

"Your friend honest, Hump?"

"He pays what he owes," Hump said.

I thought I deserved a reference too. "How about Turk?"

"He says he'll do something, he'll do it."

I shielded the deposit slip with one hand while I wrote *Her husband is looking for her.* I folded it once and waited. Across the table from me, Turk had watched the movement of my pen. Now he leaned over his slip and wrote what looked like two or three words.

"No trick?"

"No trick," I said.

We passed the slips across the table top. I opened the one that Turk had written on. It was lean to the bone and it didn't mean a thing to me.

The Parker murder. That and nothing else.

Turk read my note a time or two. "She's married?"

I didn't answer. He turned to Hump. Hump nodded.

"You didn't give me her married name."

"That wasn't part of the deal." I pushed back my chair and stood up. I lifted my almost full bottle of Bud.

"Can't say I wasn't warned." He refolded the deposit slip and stuffed it in his shirt pocket.

"You think we'll be arrested on the road for drinking?"

"Doubt it. I know my boys, they're down at the square chasing some hippie girls."

"If they catch any," I said, "make them take their shots on Monday."

We left him hunched over the table. It was cloudy and there was a light misting of rain on the windshield as we drove back toward town.

CHAPTER NINE

passed the Lakeside Motel. Next to me I saw Hump turned and leaning in that direction. "Sleepy?"

"Bloated." He turned and looked straight ahead. "We got some more business I don't know about?"

"We came all this way under the pretense of hearing some bluegrass. Thought we might take in an hour or so."

"In case Marcy asks about it?"

"Now you've got it."

It was still misting when I found a parking space some three blocks from the square. I rolled down the window and felt the cool mist on my face and listened to the thinned-out string sounds from that distance. We finished off the Buds and dropped the bottles over the seat back.

The whole three blocks we passed crowds of people heading away from the square. It didn't make much sense until I saw the fork of lightning off in the northeast. And I could feel the oppressive stillness. Which meant we were the dumb ones. The smart money was on going home.

We stepped over a barrier and we were in the square. Off to the right there was a tent with *FELKER FUNERAL HOME* on the top border. From under the tent came the smell of hot dogs grilling, hamburgers frying and the sweet scent of raw onions. Hump angled in that direction. I followed. I got a burger and something watery that was supposed to be a coke and walked out and stood with my back to a hardware store front. A five-piece band was doing "Rockytop." It was a long, long version with everybody getting a chance to step out and show something. I finished the hamburger and tossed the napkin into a trash can. I was looking around for a ledge where I could place the coke and have my hands free for applauding when another bolt of lightning sliced through the sky. It seemed to be directly behind the courthouse.

It was the signal for the heavy rain. Women screamed. People were kicking over the folding chairs. A big spotlight exploded at the side of the platform stage. The screaming got louder. And everybody ran for the awnings and the store fronts that lined the square. It was a wonder that a dozen kids didn't get stomped flat into the street.

I waited. Ten minutes and the rain didn't slacken. The stage was dark now. The thousand or so chairs, some upended, appeared to float in two or three inches of water.

Hump trotted over from the food tent. Under one arm he carried a candy box with half a dozen hot dogs stacked in it. He ate them one after another while I stared out at the rain.

It didn't look like anything was going to work out well for us in Tennessee.

The Lakeside Motel office was empty. I dumped a handful of change on the counter next to the pay phone and separated it into stacks of nickels, dimes and quarters.

I gave the long distance operator the Atlanta Police Department number and made it person-to-person to Art Maloney. I put in a dollar-twenty and listened to the call work its way up to Art's desk.

He came on, sounding hoarse and tired. "You back in town?"

"Still in Tennessee."

"Nathan Webster's been trying to reach you."

"Why?"

"How the hell do I know?" Art sounded angry. "You ask him and, while you're at it, give him a number where he can reach you. He's been worrying the hell out of me."

"I will."

"Do that."

"Art, what do you know about the Parker murder?"

"Which one?"

"I don't know."

"Where? When?"

I admitted I didn't know.

"You need to know a bit more. Otherwise I can't do one of my miracles."

That made sense. "I'll see what I can do."

"That lawyer, Carter Williams' lawyer ..."

"Markman," I said.

"He's been asking around about you," Art said.

"He find out anything?"

"Nothing but the truth," he said.

"Oh, shit."

Art hung up on me.

I replaced the receiver. I flipped pages in my notebook until I found Nathan Webster's number. A quick change count and I was fairly certain there was enough left for a station-to-station call to his house.

I poised a dime over the pay phone slot. I hesitated because I wasn't quite sure what I'd say to Webster. I heard footsteps and looked around. It was the night clerk. He was a young kid who wore cowboy boots, jeans and a fringed leather shirt. All that and he still needed a shave and a haircut. He placed a mug of coffee on the counter and reached across it and brought up a slip of paper.

"You Mr. Hardman?"

I said I was.

"I took a message for you. It came in about half an hour ago, while you were out."

I thanked him and turned the message toward me.

Emma wants to see you.

"Was it a woman's voice?"

"It sure was." From the way he looked at me I had my guess that he thought he knew who Emma was. Horny little redneck.

I winked at him and headed for the door. I was out in the breezeway before I changed my mind and went back into the office.

"Watch that, Hump."

We were on the road headed back to Thelma's. Hump had reached over and opened my jacket and felt in my waistband. It was empty. I hadn't brought anything with me. No iron. Before I could tell him that, he'd checked the glove compartment. A rattle around in there and he knew for himself.

"I'm not high on this," he said.

"A strange town and strange cops. If I'd known you were tight with the Chief, I'd have brought four or five pieces with me."

"I don't like those ifs."

There was one more bit of puzzling news he didn't know. I'd decided to keep that from him. It had hit me when I was on the breezeway.

The note: *Emma wants to see you.*

I'd walked into the motel office and leaned on the counter.

"How was the message given?"

"That way," he said. "The way I wrote it down."

"Exactly?" I asked.

"Word for word. She asked if Mr. Hardman was registered here and I said you were. She said she wanted to leave a message. That was after I tried your room and you weren't there," he told me.

"And she said Emma…?"

"Emma wants to see you. I wrote it down the way she said it," he repeated.

My headlights swept over the front of Thelma's. Two rednecks stood next to a pickup. They were passing a pint bottle of something back and forth. They turned their heads away from the light.

I parked in a spot directly in front of the motel office. The neon light still wasn't burning. There was a bright light inside and I could hear a radio playing country and western.

Hump followed me to the door. I pushed it open and stepped in. The office was empty. The bedroom beyond was dark.

"Emma?" No answer. I looked over my shoulder at Hump. "She must have stepped out for a minute."

So much for picking at words. I could feel the tightness leaving my neck and shoulders. Nobody'd tricked me into a box after all.

"You want me to wait with you, Jim?"

"Wait in the car. She doesn't know you."

"I'll do better than that. I'll see if I can scrounge up a couple of beers."

"Good thought." I closed the door behind him. I put an elbow on the counter and waited. One minute. Two minutes. I pushed away and headed for the bedroom. I found the light switch and flooded the room with strong light. The bed still unmade. A bra with rusty brown stains next to the pillow. I walked through and looked in the bathroom. A damp towel thrown over the toilet seat. A leg razor clogged with hair on the ledge of the tub.

I switched off that light and walked back into the bedroom. On the way past, I pulled open the closet door and stopped. There were a lot of empty wooden hangers. A white nightgown, the pink terrycloth robe.

I squatted and looked at the closet floor. There was a dust mark where there'd been a couple of large suitcases stored. Now gone.

I stood up. The fat bird had flown.

The rain had stopped, but the air was still damp and there was an early chill to it when I stepped out of the office and stopped under the awning.

I saw Hump in the dim light, the big dark shadow of him. He saw me, too, and he held up both hands, a bottle in each hand. He was about twenty yards away when he shouted, "Down, Jim" and drew back his right arm and threw one of the beers. At first, I thought he was playing, faking a throw to me but the *down* got to me and I turned my head and saw the shape of a man about fifteen yards off to my left. He'd stepped out of a doorway and he whirled toward me with something in his hands. It could have been a stick or a rifle or a shotgun.

I took a dive for the ground next to my Ford. I heard the loud *pop* of the beer bottle Hump had thrown and then the louder, deafening blast of a shotgun and I was rolling, rolling until the Ford shielded me. I kept my head down.

Time. Slow time. Hump leaned over me and touched my shoulder. "You all right?"

"Skinned up, I think."

He caught me under the arms and pulled me to my feet. He braced me until I got back the strength in my legs and moved away from him. I wobbled to the car and leaned against the wet hood.

"You see him, Hump?"

"Short look. He took off running." Hump twisted the cap from the remaining bottle of Bud. He offered me a swallow. "I saved one of them."

After a swallow, I looked toward the motel office. From below I could see that a big chunk of the metal awning had been blown away. I leaned against the hood of the Ford and shook. I felt like I had a chill, a hell of a fever.

CHAPTER TEN

I was over shaking by the time Turk arrived at Thelma's. I'd called the chief from the phone in the motel office and then we'd gone to Thelma's to have a beer and wait for him. We had a Bud before Turk arrived. The counterman was ready to close for the night.

He carried an old broom that was worn down to the strings when he met Turk at the front door. "Turk, I'm closing."

"Then close, dammit," Turk said, "but bring me a cold one first." Turk slumped into the chair across from me. His eyes looked red and watery. Maybe we'd awakened him while he was trying to catch some sleep at his desk. "Tell me this shit about somebody trying to kill you on my time."

"You can see the hole that got blasted..."

"Later," Turk said. "Tell me about it."

I amazed myself. I talked it to him, calm and easy. At the other side of the room, after he'd brought Turk a Bud, the counterman huffed and puffed a crazy punctuation into it while he stirred up the dust and the cigarette butts with his broom.

The two cops arrived just as I finished. Turk sent them to have a look in the motel office and to verify the shotgun damage to the awning. Turk bummed one of my Pall Malls and coughed at the first puff. "You've been in this crap before, Hardman. I can almost hear you thinking."

"I was put in a box with a ribbon on it."

"More." The second puff wasn't as bad.

I passed him the note the clerk at the Lakeside Motel had given me. Turk read it. His face didn't change. "So what?"

"*Emma* bothers me. You see, we didn't get formally introduced. I didn't know her name, and she didn't know mine. At least, I didn't know hers until you told me at the police station."

He was smart enough to see the direction I was heading. There wasn't any way I was going to make him like it. "Go on."

"Somebody messed up Christmas. They knew I'd talked to Emma, and maybe they knew I hadn't found out what I wanted to know. Just maybe on that."

"Emma?"

"I doubt it. I think she'd have remembered. Even if she'd found out my name, she'd have said *the manager of the motel behind Thelma's* or *the woman you talked to this afternoon.* Something like that." I shook my head. "I don't think she made the call. You scared the pee out of her. Or somebody did. She's flown. She's gone. And she probably won't stop for a breath before she reaches the West Coast."

"Who then?" Turk asked.

"Any woman could have made the call." I took my time. I had his attention. He'd wait. "I'm not bothered so much by the question of who made the call. I'm more interested in who set me up. That could have been you, Turk."

"It wasn't. If I'd set you up, you'd be dead. Make book on that."

The two boy cops stomped in. Ed led the way. "It's true enough, Chief," he said. "Somebody blew a hole in the sky over there."

Turk eased about in his chair and put an arm down the back of it. "Emma there?"

"No."

"Any sign she bugged out?"

That bounced back and forth between the two cops. Ed shook his head. Turk raised an eyebrow at me.

"You look in her closet?"

Ed said he hadn't.

I rubbed my eyes and looked away. "You'll find the dust out-lines where a couple of suitcases were for a long time. They're not there anymore."

"Moved recently?"

"Today, I think." I dropped my hands from my eyes. The long day was getting to me.

Turk tapped Hump on the shoulder. "Tell them about the man with the shotgun, buddy."

"White," Hump said. "About six or six-one. I didn't see his face, but there's a streak of white hair that runs up the center of his head like a paint mark."

We looked at the two kid cops.

"That fit anybody we know?" Turk said.

"Might fit two or three," Ed said.

The other cop gave Ed a puzzled look. "That's Billy Bennett."

"You get the cigar," Turk said. "He's got a shotgun?"

"An old piece of junk his daddy had. A twelve gauge."

"It shoots?"

"Last I heard. Got a deer last year."

"Where's Billy living now?" Turk explained it to Hump and me. "He sold the piece of land his daddy left him. That was five-six months ago."

Ed shook his head at the question. That done, he scratched at the acne patch with a fingernail. His eyes closed. The other cop stepped closer to Turk. "What I heard is that Billy's working shares on that north tract belongs to Mr. Ben Reed."

"The one they call Rock Farm?"

"That's what the ones that worked it call it."

"I think we ought to talk to Billy about shooting holes in motel awnings." Turk pushed back his chair. He stood up and I noticed for the first time that he was armed. He wore a stained old leather service holster and there was a .45 automatic buttoned under the flap. "You want to come along, Hump? Hardman?"

I said that we might as well.

It was hardscrabble and poor dirt land. The cropper house that went with it belonged there. The exterior walls had been built out of what looked like the waste cuts of pine. The porch was high and narrow and, in daylight, you could probably see all the way under the house and beyond. That was so the breeze, if there was one, could cool it in the summer. The winters would be bad, the way the wind would whip around under there. I guess, for these people, the way they lived, one out of two wasn't bad. It was almost a moral victory.

The porch was dark. There were lights in the house. Some of it leaked past the dime store roll-up paper shades.

The air was still damp and there was a wind blowing here and there, from this quarter and that, as if it couldn't make up its mind. By the luminous dial on my watch face, it was ten of two.

Hump and I stood, crouched over, in a four-foot ditch about forty yards from the front of the house. A thin river of water from the thunderstorm earlier in the night washed over our feet. Both my shoes were full. We'd been waiting for fifteen minutes. Off to my right, ten yards away, Turk wiped his nose on his black slicker. While the sleeves were back, he checked his watch.

It was time for his two cowboys to be in position. Ed should be at the back door. The other young cop at the front right corner of the house near the porch.

For the fifth or sixth time I looked at the .38 Police Special Turk had loaned me. He'd taken it from the trunk of the police car and casually checked the loads before he passed it to me. I didn't know the gun, and I hoped it wasn't rusted away or pitted and that the loads weren't so old they'd misfire. Strange guns make me nervous.

Hump had turned the iron down. He didn't like killing. He'd shared his first kill with Art Maloney that time in the mountains, and he'd been sick over it for weeks.

Sound at the cropper house. The front door opened and a man outlined himself in the lighted doorway. He was there long enough for us to get a slow, long look at him. He carried a shotgun with him, in the crook of his left arm. It looked long, wicked and double-barreled. Before he moved left, out of the light, I had time to check his hair. I saw the streak of gray or white hair that ran over the top of his head.

"That's the boy," Hump whispered.

Turk heard him. He dipped his head at me.

It was go down time.

I watched Turk. It was his move and I wasn't quite sure how he planned to handle it. I'd heard him position the two cops. That and nothing else. Now it was gut-it-up time or heads-down-in-the-ditch time. I knew which one it was for me. And Hump would follow my lead.

Turk reached forward, grabbed an exposed root, and pulled himself out of the ditch. He walked straight toward the porch. I could see the .45 in his hand, not pointed, loose and easy at his side.

"Who's that?"

Turk stopped. I saw the .45 move upward. "It's me, Turk. I've got to talk to you on some police business, Billy."

The cop at the right corner of the house did his part. He said, "I'm on your hip, Billy."

"Turk, you son of a bitch …."

None of it was classic. I guess you couldn't expect Billy Bennett to follow a bad script either. Maybe it was the way the full moon affected people in Tennessee.

"Billy, it's just some talk we want," Turk said.

Billy made a running dive for the open, lighted doorway. He was in the light for a split second, rolling and twisted, and he kicked the door closed behind him. He'd kept the shotgun with him and I stepped out of the ditch, the .38 at the ready.

Turk hesitated and I came level with him. He waved me around the left side of the house. I saw him head straight for the front steps. I ducked and trotted toward the back of the house. I'd gone about ten yards when I heard the *whomp-whomp* of a shotgun. I stopped. Turk, who'd been on the steps, sprinted past me.

"Ed, you sing out."

"I got him, Turk. I'm all right."

Turk ran on. He could still move. I settled to a walk. By the time I reached the back steps, the two young cops and Turk formed a half-circle around the body of Billy Bennett. Two heavy-duty flashlights lit up the body. I only needed one look. He'd taken two hits. One had torn up his chest. The other had blown away the top of his head.

I could hear the shuddering breath from Ed. "I do the right thing, Turk?"

Turk put a foot on the bottom back step. "You call out to him?

"It didn't do any good up front," Ed said.

"You tell him to stop?"

"I called his name," Ed said, "and he turned the shotgun toward me."

"You whisper?"

I skirted the body. The shotgun was on the ground next to him. I picked up the shotgun. I couldn't be sure in the dark, but I thought it was an old Iver Johnson with the exposed hammers. I fumbled with the catch and opened it. I used a finger to check the chambers. Empty, no shells in it. I reached out and took the flashlight from the young cop whose name I didn't know. I worked it around the area. Near Billy Bennett's left hand, I found a scattering of shells. Before I returned the flashlight, I moved it over my hands. I'd picked up slick palms from the oil.

I walked up the back steps and into the house. The smell of the cleaning oil was stronger in there. The open bottle of oil, the rod and the cleaning patches were on the kitchen table. There was an open box of shells on the kitchen sink. Five or six shells were left in the box. I read the label. Double-o buckshot.

Steps behind me on the plank floor. Turk leaned past me and looked at the shells. "That's nasty stuff," he said.

I nodded. Double-o could cure hangnails, bad breath and the clap all at once.

It was three-thirty-five by my watch.

Turk lined up three paper cups on the night table and cracked the seal on the bottle of J&B. He sat on the edge of my bed and poured fist-like shots. I sipped mine and held Hump's for him until he came out of the bathroom where he'd been washing up. It was that kind of night. I looked down at what had been at one time a good pair of summer pants. I looked like I'd been digging in a clay pit.

"This hair won't scratch you," Turk said.

I could feel him watching me. It had been that way on the drive from Rock Farm to Thelma's where I'd picked up my Ford. We'd agreed to meet at the motel room for a drink. Now it had started up again. A close, tight watch like he was trying to read my mind. That walk around wasn't necessary. All he had to do was ask. I'd be glad to tell him.

"You still bothered, Hardman?"

"That cowboy of yours, after he goes back to work at the garage, he ain't going to work on my car."

"That's what's burning you?"

"This dead-end," I said. "I might as well be back in Atlanta."

"That's a good idea," Turk said.

I grinned at Hump. "You think the chief is telling us to leave town?"

"Nothing like that," Turk said, "but I've got a feeling it's going to rain out the festival tomorrow, too."

"I'll make one more deal with you." I held out the cup and he tipped a couple of shots into it. "You tell me about the Parker murder and I'll leave the beautiful town of Backwater, Tennessee, with no regrets."

"Tell me about some husband married to Ellen Carver or Cora Abse or whatever. Give me his name."

"Bad memory," I said. It was a standoff.

"Oh, shit. Maybe you leaving town is worth it. I'll tell you this much. Parker lived in Gaptown, and he lived there until 1968."

"That's Gaptown, Tennessee?"

"Right by the Georgia line," Turk said.

"What was Ellen Carver's part in the murder?"

"Who said she had any part in anything? Look, it's a dirty mess and people have been raking in it for years. I'm not about to put my rake in that barnyard crap."

"Telling me about it you've done it."

"How?" He put the cap on the J&B. "The facts are all there. You'd find out which Parker murder it was. You've got that many brains." He stood up and stretched. "You two leaving in the morning?"

"Might as well. Ellen Carver's left town."

"Gone where?"

I smiled at him.

"Jesus Christ, I just ..." He stopped. "You in the Atlanta phone book?"

"I'm there."

"Tomorrow's a busy day. If it don't rain the damned thing out, I've got to police all those hippies and all those fat-assed tourists. Sunday or Monday, I plan to have a talk with Ed Beuller."

"The cowboy?"

He nodded.

"Knuckle talk?" Hump said.

"If I have to," Turk said. "You see, I've been listening to you and I don't like the smell of this."

I kicked off my muddy shoes. "And after you talk to Ed, you're going to call me and tell me what you found out?"

"Maybe. Maybe not."

Hump followed him to the door and they shook hands, and Turk talked about coming to Atlanta some day for a drink and to see a Falcon game. Hump closed the door behind him and locked it and started undressing. "It ain't going to hurt my feelings any to leave this town."

"Ditto," I said. I threw my muddy socks against the wall. "Double ditto."

I couldn't sleep. I was rolling from side to side. At seven I gave it up and stumbled out of bed. I turned on the overhead light and began dressing. Hump didn't like it, but he decided to go along when I said he could have the back seat.

While Hump stored the bags in the car, I settled up at the motel office. The kid with the cowboy boots and the leather fringed jacket was still on duty. I paid him and walked out to the breezeway. I took a last look at the lake or river or whatever it was behind the motel.

The kid followed me and stood in the doorway. "One thing I didn't remember to tell you yesterday about that call. The woman asked where you were from."

"And you told her?"

"What was on the registration card," he said. "The street address and Atlanta. That's right, isn't it?"

I nodded. That was right enough.

CHAPTER ELEVEN

When I cut the engine, Hump sat up in the back seat. His eyes looked like he had been in a dust storm, and he groaned when he tried to stretch out his legs. That back seat wasn't designed to sleep even a six-foot man. It was cramped hell on six-six or six-seven.

"We there already?"

I looked over the seat back at him. "This look or smell like Atlanta?"

He sniffed. "It's not the right smell."

It didn't look like Atlanta, either. Gaptown is a narrow little resort town. The four or so blocks show nothing but motels and cafes and junk-gift shops and a number of auction shops. The auction shops specialize in old silver and furniture. I didn't do a count, but I figured there were about as many as you'd find in Blowing Rock, North Carolina during the tourist season.

I'd parked next to a white MG with battered fenders and rust beginning to show around the dings and dents. From the car I could read the lettering in the window of the low wood frame building.

THE GAPTOWN SENTRY

THE SOUTH'S FINEST WEEKLY

The building, some time in the past, might have been one of those Ma and Pa grocery stores. I got the clue from the *fancy groc* in the chipping paint up near the roof line.

Out of the car, I waited while Hump limped and stomped the feeling back into his legs. I spent that time looking up at the mountains that seemed to hunch and lean toward the town. The mountains were rounded and old, treed over and almost blue-green in the spring chill before noon.

I tried the door. It was locked. That was me. Never read the sign until afterwards. *At Breakfast. Back in half an hour.* A lot of good that did. When was the half hour up?

The notice was signed in a flowing script, *J. Giles.*

"Cafe right there," Hump said.

I followed the swing of his arm and found it. A blue and yellow brick front with glass all the way around. *FAN'S COUNTRY COOKING.*

"Assuming this is his car ..."

"And assuming it runs," Hump said.

"We ought to find Mr. Giles there face down in his oatmeal."

"Detective work is fun," Hump said.

We took the booth near the front entrance. There was a good smell to the place. The scent of freshly-made biscuits, what you couldn't fake, the flour dusty smell, and the salty aroma of frying, salt-cured ham. This kind of place you could probably get red-eye gravy with your grits.

Hump read the menu while I looked over the other diners. A slow look about and I was certain I'd picked him out. A gray-haired, almost emaciated man in his late fifties sat alone at a booth in the back corner. He was reading the Nashville paper as he ate. One forkful and he'd read a paragraph, then another bite and another paragraph.

It was the two-hour breakfast the way he went at it.

The waitress brought our coffee and took our orders. Before she stepped away, I asked if Mr. Giles was in the cafe.

"There." She tilted her head toward the counter.

"Where?"

"There."

The man she indicated was in his middle twenties. He wore flared, green-checked slacks, boots with Cuban heels and a blue alpaca sweater. He wasn't at all my idea of what a small-town editor was supposed to look like.

I had a sip of the coffee and slid out of the booth. I carried my cup to the counter and sat down on the stool next to Giles. "You the editor of the Sentry?"

The swing toward me was almost slow motion. I knew why when I saw the ravaged face and the bleak eyes. Mr. Giles had been too close to the bottle the night before. Before he could answer me, the counter waitress brought him half a glass of water and a foil package of Alka-Seltzer. His hands shook as he struggled with the pack. He broke one tablet trying to get it out of the package and into the glass. Only after it was fizzing did he turn to me again.

"I'm John Giles."

"I'm James Hardman from Atlanta."

"That must be nice."

"What?"

"Being away from Atlanta."

I smiled. It wasn't that good, but I wanted something from him and if he considered himself a wit, I'd try my best to humor him. "It's good to breathe some fresh air."

"That's what we've got here," he said. "And damn little else." He lifted the glass in both hands and poured it back in one long swallow. He wiped the back of a hand across his mouth. "You want to see me about something?"

Lie time. "I've been doing some writing, just freelance stuff. Mainly magazine ..."

"I can save you the trouble. I don't have an opening."

"It's not that," I said. "I'm thinking about doing a book. Non-fiction is big now. Fiction's dead. A friend suggested I look into something here. I'll do a proposal and he'll send it to his editor at Random House."

"And try for a contract, huh?"

I nodded. "It works that way."

"And you want some information from me?"

"It would be a big help."

"Stop me if I'm wrong…"

No reason to be coy. And the best lies are the ones with a tablespoon of honesty in them. "It's the Parker murder," I said.

"I thought so. You're not the first."

The waitress placed a buttered english muffin and a cup of tea next to Giles' elbow. He played dip-the-tea-bag and waited me out. It was my move.

"What are the chances?"

"Could be," he said.

"I'd like to look over the back issues, the ones that cover the murder."

"I've got one question." He mashed the teabag between his thumb and the spoon and dropped the bag on the saucer. "Are you keeping a close expense account?"

"Huh?"

"You putting down your research expenses?"

"Sure," I said. Whatever that meant. I knew what it meant to him. I had a feeling.

"My time's worth something," he said.

I told him that I understood. "How long do you think it would take me to go back over the files?"

"An hour, more or less. It would take a longer time, but I've done the clipping. I'm about to do a retrospective on the case. You know, seven years afterwards, that kind of thing."

"What's your time worth?" I looked at my booth. Hump was already into his breakfast.

"On the low side," he said, "about twenty dollars an hour."

"I think I can bury that in the expense sheet somewhere."

"I thought you could."

He appeared to be watching my hands, waiting for it, so I got out my roll and held it under the counter level and worked a twenty free. I folded it a couple of times and slid it across the counter until it was hidden by the saucer. His hand covered it like he was trapping flies.

I said I'd be over after I had breakfast.

He said he'd have the package out and waiting.

Greeds, the small ones, the petty ones. Whoring for a bill or two.

I kept my face over my plate a few minutes later when he left the cafe and headed across the street to the newspaper office.

Hump watched him cross the street. "It set?"

I said that it was.

An hour later, we left Gaptown and headed for Atlanta.

Hump had the wheel. I locked the passenger door and pressed my face against the window and tried to sleep. It got warm and I couldn't sleep and forms like misshapen animals danced behind my eyelids.

I hadn't taken any notes. I hadn't needed to. There were some things you could remember, like your social security number or the first time you got laid.

It began that Sunday morning the first week in June of 1968. The Gaptown police received a call from an elderly lady in the Crown Heights section of town. The lady said she thought she'd heard gunfire at the Asa M. Parker estate across the road.

"When was that?"

"An hour ago," the lady said.

Asked why she'd waited an hour before she'd called the police, the lady said that she hadn't been really certain it was gunfire at first, and she'd about convinced herself that it wasn't when she'd heard tires screech on the road and she'd looked out her front window. A dark car, she wasn't sure what make, had roared out of the Parker driveway and sped away toward the Interstate.

"How long ago was that?"

"Half an hour," she'd said. It had taken her that long to decide to call Asa Parker. He hadn't answered and that was when she'd phoned the police.

The police reached the Parker house in five minutes. The first sign that something was wrong was the body of the dead Doberman on the front porch. It had been shot a couple of times. A trail of blood spots led from the front porch to the living room. A bloody towel in the downstairs bathroom and another torn into strips pointed to the probability that the Doberman had bitten someone before it was killed.

There was a perfectly preserved heelprint from a woman's shoe in the blood on the tile floor of the bathroom.

Police found the body of Asa Parker in the upstairs bedroom. He'd been shot several times. The last shot, the kill one, had been fired into the back of his head at close range.

A wall safe above the bed had been opened. Papers from the safe had been scattered all across the bed and the bedroom floor.

And that was all. No fingerprints. No real leads.

Outrage colored the language of the articles that first month or so. Editorials deplored the inactivity of the police. Rewards were offered. And nothing came of it.

The Parker case faded from the front pages. There were no more promises of an early solution.

Asa M. Parker, the retired dentist from Dayton, Ohio, was almost forgotten.

"It freaks me some," Hump said. "That the girl had hooked some, that didn't bother me. But this..."

"Too rank for you?"

"This is a job I want to quit," Hump said. "That girl can stay lost."

In December of 1968, some seven months or so after the murder of Asa Parker, a nineteen-year-old girl named Cora Abse is living in Nashville. She doesn't have a job, has no visible means of support, yet she lives in a $250 a month apartment and drives a late model Buick.

Cora Abse shoplifts a $32 bottle of perfume at a downtown department store. And she is caught. When Cora Abse is arrested, she has over five hundred dollars in her purse. It was probably boredom that prompted it. Boredom and the need for some kind of cheap thrill.

While in jail, she develops a friendship with a young, uniformed policeman. He talks to her and brings her cigarettes and helps her with the bail procedure. After she is released, he continues to see her. One night, though the circumstances are clouded, Cora Abse brags that she can finger the men who robbed and killed Asa Parker. She even convinces him that she is the woman whose heelprint was found at the scene of the crime.

The young policeman falls by the way. He has served his purpose. An investigator from the Tennessee Bureau replaces him. Two days of talks and she gives him the names of the three men. A deal is hammered out. The shoplifting charge will be dropped and she will be given immunity if she testifies against the other three.

Two of the men Cora Abse names are already in prison. Ben Lipmann and Arnold Schmidt had been arrested as part of a car theft ring in Knoxville and are doing two-to-five. The third man, Chris Morton, they find working construction in Macon.

The parts fall together. Ben Lipmann has a recent scar on his right arm. He argues that the scar is from a swimming accident, that he'd cut the arm on a submerged can. He has no proof of this.

It is a long trial. The prosecution's whole case is Cora Abse. Her testimony lasts three days. She tells about living with Ben Lipmann, about how she left Smythtown. She recounts a number of other jobs that she'd participated in with Lipmann, Schmidt and Morton. And she breaks down and weeps on the stand when she tells about being forced to fire the kill shot into the back of Asa Parker's head. It was, she says, their way of insuring that she'd never fink on them.

The defense cross-examination lasts four days. They can not shake her basic story.

The trial is over by the spring of 1969. The three men are sentenced to life imprisonment. Cora Abse, released, disappears in some direction or other.

"Jim?"

I opened my eyes and straightened up. The right side of my face was numb from the pressure against the car window. "Yeah?"

"I've got a feeling."

"Tell me about it."

"That's a black Capri back of us. It's been with us since we left Gaptown."

"Sure?"

"I'm sure."

A blue pickup wagged tail around us. I looked at the dash. Hump was doing about forty. The black Capri kept the distance.

"I've been dogging it," Hump said. "I've given them every chance to pass and they won't."

Light traffic on the road. I saw a sign coming up. REST STOP 1 MILE.

"We out of Tennessee yet?"

"Ten miles from the line," Hump said.

I pointed at the sign. "Let's take a break."

There was only one car in the parking lot next to the rest center. A family had spread a picnic lunch on a grassy rise some distance away from the main building.

I led the way to the men's room. At the door, I looked around and saw the black Capri swing into the space to the left of my Ford. Two men stepped out. I pushed the door in and we were in the otherwise empty rest room.

"The wall by the door," I said to Hump.

Hump moved there and flattened himself against the tile wall.

I turned on the water at the nearest wash basin. I was about three steps from the door. I didn't bother to wet my hands. I pulled out a wad of paper towels and waited.

They came in fast and together. The first one through the door had a pale blondish mustache and wore a plaid summer jacket. It was unbuttoned and he was reaching for his hip when Hump saw my nod and swung away from the wall. He hit that one against the side of the head. He fell to the floor and slid across the tile floor until he was halfway under the door to one of the enclosed booths.

The second man was older. He wore a blue blazer and I noticed the salt sprinkling of dandruff on his shoulders when I swung a right at him. He said, "Wait, we're..."

It was too late. I hit him belly-high. His breath *whoosed* at me. He was falling when Hump hit him against the ear and flipped him.

Both were down and out. I leaned over the older one, the one in the blue blazer, and turned him over on his back. As I'd figured, he was carrying a short barrel .38 in a belt holster. I dug into the inside jacket pocket and pulled out a wallet. Along with that came the flat leather ID case.

I held the case in my hand for a few seconds. There were a number of possibilities, and none of them were good. And some of them were less good than others.

I opened the case. Tennessee Bureau of Investigation. I stuffed the wallet and the ID case back in the coat pocket. I straightened up. Hump stood by the door. He was rubbing the knuckles on his right hand.

"What is it?"

"We just beat up a couple of cops."

"What now?"

"You kidding?" I headed for the door.

Ten minutes later we crossed the border into Georgia.

With the Atlanta skyline ahead Hump said, "I feel like I'm back in Paradise. Smell that pollution, smell those bars with real booze in them."

I nodded. But I didn't quite agree. If it was Paradise, it was Eden a few hours after the snake came to town.

CHAPTER TWELVE

"You did what?"

"You heard me," I said. "I don't stutter."

Art jacked himself out of his seat on the sofa, stepped over the coffee table and gave the on-off switch of the TV a jerk that almost broke the knob. "You know...you know they're going to..." He sputtered. I could see the spray of spit bubble over his bottom lip. "God dammit, Jim."

"Hear me out." I shook out a smoke and lit it and blew the smoke at him. "Let me tell you how Hump and I spent our spring vacation."

"Is it a short story?" He looked at his watch. "Is it a short, short story?"

I said it wasn't.

"I'd better check in."

I heard him call in. He said he was going off for supper, and he gave my number if anything important came up in the next half hour or so.

It was Saturday night. We'd been in town, back from Tennessee, for two or three hours. Hump had gone home to shower and nap for a time. Marcy was out, and I didn't know how to reach her. I'd decided I'd better try to cover my rear end. Dumb idea. It was like Art, even before he knew all the facts, to get upset because we'd left two T.B.I. cops banged up in that john just over the state line.

"From the beginning," Art said, "and don't leave out the bad parts."

"They were all bad." I stubbed out the smoke and passed him on the way to the kitchen. "You drinking?"

"If a sandwich comes with it. You're wasting my supper time."

I waved him into the kitchen. I nodded at the refrigerator and sat down at the kitchen table. I talked my way through the first part of the story, the time in Smythtown, while Art chewed a path through about half my package of deli corned beef. By the time I'd reached the Gaptown episode and the bribing of the newspaper editor, he was digging in the refrigerator again.

"What are you looking for?"

"Dessert," he said.

"I don't have any."

"No pie? No cake?"

"Nothing." I watched him settle into his chair once more. He picked at a thick wad of swiss cheese. He chipped away at it while I gave him a rundown on the Parker murder.

"That Parker murder," Art said. "I remember some of it." He closed the foil wrap over the cheese and pushed it away from him. "You sure it's the same girl?"

"Yeah." There'd been pictures in the papers. She'd been younger then, and she'd had dirty blonde hair. Maybe the beauty operators in that part of the world didn't have much taste, but you couldn't change the basic facial features. "Cora Abse is Ellen Carver is Ellen Webster."

"Go on with it."

I took my time over the run-in with the T.B.I. cops.

"You thought they were reaching, you say?"

"It looked that way to me. Look, if they were cops and they wanted to talk to us, why didn't they just pull us to the side of the road and get it done?"

"Good question." Art drained the foam from the bottle of Bud and tapped it on the table top thoughtfully. "If they didn't pull you, they must have had a reason."

"Give me one."

He shrugged. "You couldn't have been a bit slower?"

"After the shotgun try in Smythtown?"

"You hurt them bad?" Art stood up and belched.

"Lumps and bruises."

Art stopped in the doorway. "You got mouthwash?"

"In the bathroom."

I cleared the table and dropped the plate and the silverware in the sink. It was taking Art a long time to lose his beer breath. I soft-stepped to the bedroom doorway and leaned in. Art was on the phone.

"They've been here how long? How do they look?"

Art lifted his head and found me listening. He shook his head slowly from side-to-side.

"Look, have them hold off on that crap until I've talked to them. I know a bit about the circumstances. We talk some and it might not be necessary. Might be we can work out something."

I made my guess. I circled the bed and got a jacket from the closet.

"Get them a cup of coffee and tell them I'll be there in twenty minutes." He replaced the receiver. "Your trouble is in town, Jim."

"I figured."

"They've been threatening extradition to Captain Wade."

"Wade would give me to them as a Crackerjack prize if it was on his say." I put on the jacket. "I'll go down with you."

"Not yet. I'll talk to them alone first and see if I can't do some stroking."

"If you can … ?" left it hanging for him.

"If I can or if I can't, it's all the same. You're going to have to talk to them."

"That the only choice I've got?"

"It ain't no choice at all," Art said. "You be here."

I phoned Hump. He arrived fifteen minutes later. He brought a fifth of J&B. We had half an hour to forty minutes to numb the worry away.

⚜ ⚜ ⚜

The young cop, the one with the thin pale mustache, had a scrape on the left side of his face. I guess you could call it tile burn from the slide he'd taken. The right side of his jaw was puffy and swollen. Hump had one-punched him pretty well. He was going to be doing a lot of left-jawed chewing the next week or two.

The older cop had changed his coat. The dandruff didn't show as much against the tan material, but I knew it was still there. His right ear looked like a thick slice of ripe beefsteak tomato.

Neither of the two, seated stiffly shoulder-to-shoulder on my sofa, showed much of a friendly attitude. They'd passed up the offer of the scotch, and they'd taken a beer only after Art had. One swallow and they'd pushed the bottles toward the far side of the coffee table.

The older cop, Vincent, said, "I've been in touch with the Governor's office, and the request for extradition can be hand-carried here to Atlanta by noon tomorrow. We can start action on it Monday."

"At the least you'll do a year," the young cop, Barstow, said.

I listened to them, but I was watching Art's face. It was too Irish to hide much. The concern wasn't there. The T.B.I. cops could have been talking sports or cars from the reaction Art gave. So, I read it this way: Art was saying, these Tennessee boys are going to sound mean and tough, they're going to show you the cards they have, but under all that they think they need you, and if they think that, then it's a trade-off.

I decided if that was my choice, I'd better accept it. "What is it you want?"

"We want Cora Abse or Ellen Carver or whatever her name is now."

"Maybe you can tell me what you want with her."

At first, I thought I'd pushed it too hard without giving anything in return. I saw Art's motion, a slight shake of his head. But the T.B.I. men crossed eyeballs for a few seconds before the older cop, Vincent, said, "Tell him about it."

Barstow, picking at his mustache now and then, spread it out for us.

Three months before, in late February, a man named Jim Martin, who was doing two life terms for the rape-murder of a waitress in Dothan, Alabama, passed the word from his cell in Huntsville Prison. He said he'd taken part in the Asa Parker murder. The T.B.I. crossed over into Alabama to talk to him. It wasn't that Martin had found religion or anything like that. He had a mad on against the two men who'd been with him that Sunday morning in Gaptown. He believed he hadn't been treated right in the split, and he was upset because he was doing hard time while the others were out on the pavement. So far, the T.B.I, didn't have the names of the two men or the woman who'd been involved. Jim Martin wanted an impossible deal before he'd name them. It was impossible because he wanted the same kind of immunity that had been given Cora Abse. And Alabama wasn't so interested in solving Tennessee murders that they'd make any deal about the two life terms he was serving. It was a standoff.

Martin hinted that the identity of one of the men would surprise them. And he had a jagged scar on his left forearm that could have been from the Doberman bite, and he knew some of the details of the murder that hadn't been given publicity. Check points, the T.B.I. man called them.

So, Tennessee was between a brick wall and some hard places. Three men had done about six years in prison. Whatever these three men deserved for their other crimes, there was the chance that they'd done time for a crime they hadn't committed. The State was thinking of re-opening the case. Before that, they needed to talk to the star witness, Cora Abse or Ellen Carver. If Jim Martin was telling the truth, if he wasn't trying to lie his ex-friends into jail, then the witness had perjured herself. Or Martin was lying and the witness had told the truth.

"You lost track of her?" I said.

"We didn't have a rope on her," Vincent said. "It was complete immunity. And six years, that's a long time to backtrack. Hell, she could have left the country for all we knew. We'd about decided that we'd never find her until you two blundered into Smythtown and started asking questions."

"You knew about the name change?"

He nodded. "That was part of the deal. A new name and a new identity."

"Turk Edwards called you?"

"This morning early. He said he thought you were headed for Gaptown. And he gave us your tag numbers."

"Good buddy, Turk," I said to Hump.

Hump said, "He's changed."

"We got to Gaptown while you were having breakfast. We were set to follow you to Maine if we had to."

"But you changed your mind?"

"You got cute," Barstow said. "That slowing down to see if we were a tail. It made sense to collar you before you got over the state line."

"When you talked to Turk, he told you about the try on me?"

"He told me," Vincent said.

"Maybe you can understand why we got nervous."

Vincent raised a hand and cupped the swollen ear. He wasn't going to be that understanding. "Maloney told us how you felt." That was as far as he'd go.

"Just a minute." I returned from the bedroom with the three photos of Ellen Webster. I dropped them, one by one, on the coffee table. "This is how she looks now."

"Changed her hair color and wears it longer," Vincent said.

"Lost her baby fat," Barstow said.

While they studied the pictures, I went back into the bedroom and closed the door behind me. I dialed Nathan Webster's number.

He had a burn on. He said, "Where have to been? You were supposed to call…?"

I cut him off. "Can you come over to my place?"

"Right now?"

"Soon as you can."

"You've found her?"

"It's something else," I said. "It's out of my hands."

He didn't understand that. I could feel the confusion. I broke the connection. More talk wouldn't help.

Hump and I sat on the stone wall that shores up the terrace garden. We'd taken a bucket of ice, glasses and the rest of the J&B along for company.

It was a clear spring night. Dogs barked off in the distance. One to the east, another in the south. Then silence. It was chilly. I'd shivered some, but I'd suffered it rather than going in the house for a sweater. In there, in that living room, I knew there were guts and tripe all over the floor. Webster's insides and all the tender inner parts stomped on. It wasn't something I wanted to see. No matter how I felt about Webster.

We drank the J&B and watched the lights down below. We talked Braves for a time, and there was the quarterback the Falcons had picked up in the draft the year before. And the Flames, the last time we'd seen them, still weren't skating the whole match.

All that so we wouldn't hear, deep in our guts, what was being said. Or the silent screams, the ones that wouldn't draw a crowd on a street. The ones that had the death grunt at the end of them.

"Fuck it," I said. "Fuck it."

"What?

"All of it."

"All of what?"

I shook my head and drank from the bottle.

By my watch, they'd been at it fifty-one minutes. I heard car doors slam, and the dog off in the south barked, and the car engine roared in front of my house, and I knew it was over for the time.

"Looks like those good old boys from Tennessee left," Hump said.

"They'll be back." I edged off the wall and touched ground with my feet. I stood there, letting the dizziness pass, and the back door opened, and Art came out. Nathan Webster was a step behind him.

Art reached us first and leaned a hip against the wall. "They'll be in town a few days."

"Figured it," I said.

"And they accepted your apology. There won't be any try at extradition."

"What apology?"

"The implied one," Art said.

"Oh, that one?"

Maybe there was something in my voice. I didn't hear the slur, but Art must have. He leaned close to me and looked into my face. "You'd better get to bed, Jim."

"I'm fine," I said.

Art looked over his shoulder at Hump. "Hump?"

"If the man says he's fine then it is a fact that the man is fine."

"You two." Art said goodnight and stumbled down the slope and around the side of the house toward the driveway. Nathan Webster stood a few feet down the slope from us, and he said a soft goodnight to Art. I couldn't see Webster's face. His chin was pressed down into his breastbone.

It was quiet and still again, and I could hear some small animal rattling around in the wood on the other side of the terrace. Headlights streaked up the drive as Art started up his car. The light curled away as he backed out.

"Do you believe those things?"

I didn't need to see his face. I didn't want to see his face. I said, yes, I believed most of it. There were blank spots in there, gaps, but there seemed to be a base of fact in what we'd learned in the last couple of days.

He moved closer. A step and then another one. "It's just … not like … anything I know about her."

The anger was deep in the bone, part of the marrow. "Who the shit ever really knows anybody anyway?"

It was three a.m. talk before midnight. To my left, Hump fidgeted and cleared his throat. I waited, but he didn't say anything.

"I want to talk to her before those men do," Webster said.

"It won't do any good," I said. "Write it off, piss on it."

"I can't do that. I just can't."

"That's the best advice you're going to get this year," Hump said.

"I don't want advice."

Clouds moved between us and the moon. The chill wind had me shivering again. Or the words did. I rubbed my bare arms and felt the hair up, like wire.

"You know what my mother said about Ellen?"

I waited. I knew he'd tell us.

"She said Ellen was a tramp, that she was cheap and tacky, that she would use me and leave me."

"Your mother always right?" Hump planted his feet solidly and stretched.

"She thinks she is. This time, I don't want her to be."

It wasn't going anywhere. Round and round and round like a squirrel I'd seen dying in the street just seconds after it had been hit by a car. I didn't want any more of it.

"I've cashed your check. I'll do some figuring tomorrow and see what the trip to Tennessee cost. I'll return what's left of the thousand. If your wife's in town, Art will find her. That's free. You don't want any advice. I've got one piece more. Take the money, and make a down payment on a lawyer. I've got a feeling your wife's going to need one."

"I don't want you to quit. That's not what I want. I still want you to find Ellen. I have to talk to her."

He couldn't say it, but I knew. All the past had hit him, the hooking, the possible involvement in a murder, that whole black life before he had met her. That hurt him, stunned him, chipped parts of him away. I had one more look at him. Maybe I'd misread him. Maybe he had more guts than I'd thought. And I knew what he wanted to ask Cora Abse-Ellen Carver-Ellen Webster. Smack in the face, right out front. Were the five years of the marriage a complete lie?

"All right," I said. "I can't speak for Hump, but I'll give it a day or two more."

"What's another day or two out of a lifetime?" Hump said.

He thanked us and left. We left the glasses and the ice bucket on the wall. Morning would be soon enough for that. Hump carried what was left of the bottle. I slumped into a kitchen chair. Hump put on some water for coffee.

"That's one miserable bastard there," he said.

"It's like one time I smoked dope."

"You? Straight you?"

"I was trying to impress this girl. Going to get a little high with her and say all kinds of sweet candy things to her. There were five or six of us, and the joints started passing around and it must have been the world's strongest shit. Suddenly, no warning, and I was numb and stoned. I couldn't even talk. I couldn't even blink. I just sat there with that dumb look on my face, and I knew that the way I felt was from the first two or three tokes. And I thought I was going to die, because there were still about three more tokes that hadn't hit me yet."

"That confession means ... ?"

"It's a metaphor," I said. "Webster doesn't know it yet, but there's a damned good chance there are about three or four more licks he's going to get hit with that he doesn't expect."

"You do any good with that girl?"

I said I hadn't. He grinned at me and made the coffee.

I couldn't sleep.

At three, I gave up and got out of bed and had a couple of Alka-Seltzers. I sat on the edge of the bed for a time and waited to see if the aspirin in it would relax me any. Not that I could tell. I was still wide awake. I put on my slippers and checked the front yard for the morning paper. It hadn't been delivered yet.

Still, desolate time. I sat at the kitchen table and blinked at the overhead light.

All those loose ends fluttering in my mind. The gaps and the blank places.

One. Start with someone trying to have Nathan Webster killed and getting killed himself. Was Cora-Ellen involved in that? If not, who was?

Two. The Smythtown and Gaptown visits that opened up that spoiled can of peas. The try on me. Was any of that, the past and the present, tied to the conspiracy to murder in Atlanta?

Three. Was it one big ball of wax or two balls? All wrapped together or separate, not touching and not supposed to touch?

I had a glass of milk and blinked and yawned.

Loose ends and gaps and blanks.

I rinsed the glass and tried the bed again. Just as I dropped off to sleep, I heard the newspaper hit the front steps.

CHAPTER THIRTEEN

I slept late Sunday morning. Ragged nerve ends from the J&B. I thought about how much worse I'd have felt if I hadn't dosed myself with Alka-Seltzer at three a.m. Coughing and hacking from the cigarettes and watching the brown phlegm washed down the wash basin.

Better by noon. A coating of milk soothed my stomach. I was risking all that comfort with a cup of coffee when my first visitor for the day arrived.

Marcy used her key to let herself in the front door. She tiptoed to the bedroom, saw the rumpled bed and drifted back to the kitchen. "I wasn't sure you'd be back yet, Jim."

"Checking my bed for fat ladies?"

"Of course." The coffee water was still hot. Marcy found a cup and stirred some of the instant powder in. "How was the bluegrass?"

"It was called on account of rain and terror and double-zero buckshot."

"All of it?" She sat down across from me.

"I heard 'Rockytop' once," I said. "It was great."

Her eyes searched my face. "You don't look well."

"It's just another Sunday. Like any other Sunday."

"That explains it all. How were the girls in Tennessee?"

"The one I got interested in almost got me killed."

The curiosity dripped toward the edge of her tongue. Before she could ask her question, Art rapped the back door a couple of times and let himself in. He looked at Marcy and at me. Marcy gave him a brief hug and pointed him toward the end chair. "Coffee, Art?"

"Thanks."

"She just got here," I said. "Stop seeing sin everywhere."

Marcy said, "Shut up, Jim."

"You're up early, Art." I grinned at Marcy. That would show her.

"I haven't been to bed yet. I started to call you last night."

"Glad you didn't."

"You'd have been interested if your brains weren't scrambled. Something came in. An abandoned blue VW."

"Right tag numbers?"

"YAG 341," Art said.

"Where?"

"On Morningside."

"That was fast."

"It was a fluke," Art said. He thanked Marcy with a nod when she placed a cup of instant in front of him. He had a sip. "Might not have located it so soon except for one thing. You know how it is with abandoned cars. Mainly there's a three or four day wait to see if it's moved before we have it towed. This one, the dumbass, parked it next to a fire hydrant. The patrolman who found it called in the tag numbers. I'd put them on a sheet. They matched. The report was on my desk when I got back to the department from here last night."

"So she's back in town?"

"Maybe. Maybe not. After they towed it in, I had a look at it." He shrugged. "It was a slow night."

At the stove, Marcy dropped half a package of bacon into the skillet. Good for her. She was starting breakfast. "You had breakfast yet, Art?"

"Not yet," Art said. Then back to me. "Found a spent shotgun casing rolled under the seat. That started me thinking."

"And?"

"On a hunch, I had the dash and the steering wheel dusted. Some of the prints were Ellen Webster's. That's usual. Some others weren't. Had enough prints to check them through the network. I put a hurry on it. Just got the word back. The prints, most of them off the steering wheel, belong to a woman named Betty Franklin, also known as Betsy Frank, also known as Emma Terry, also known as ..."

I stopped him. "Emma Terry? Mainly arrests for hooking, things involved with that?"

"How'd you know?"

"Give me a minute." I carried my coffee into the bedroom. I worked my way through information and got the police station in Smythtown. He wasn't there and the call passed on to his house.

"Yeah?"

"Jim Hardman in Atlanta."

"I said I *might* call you," he said.

"It's not that. Emma, the madam at the Castel Motel ... she have a last name?"

"She's had a lot of them."

"The latest one?"

"Terry. Why?"

"Later." I said I'd get back to him and hung up.

I sat on the edge of the bed and let it sift through. Some of it fitted and some of it didn't. The parts that didn't fit probably meant that I didn't know enough yet.

Back across the table from Art, I said, "Terry's the last name of the madam at the motel where the try was made."

"But what the hell ..."

I closed my eyes. My head didn't want to work. "Anything else in the VW?"

"Some clothes. Atlanta store labels."

I shook my head.

"Somebody'd been messy in the back seat. Had tracked in some clay. Big clumps that might have been on shoe soles."

That was the nail in the box. I think I knew then and the bottom of my stomach dropped out. "That's it."

"That's what?"

Marcy placed plates of scrambled eggs and bacon on the table. Art didn't wait for my answer. He started eating. But his eyes remained fixed on me.

"You know how to get in touch with the T.B.I. men, Vincent and Barstow?"

"They're at Stouffer's on West Peachtree."

"When you finish eating, give them a call," I said. I pulled the plate closer and looked down at it.

"And say what?"

"That I know where Ellen Webster is."

"You mean you've got a guess?"

I shook my head. "I'm dead sure."

I forked a small dab of egg and swallowed it. There. Stay down.

Rock Farm was even uglier and bleaker in daylight. It was late afternoon. There were four of us and the heavy equipment operator and his digger. The operator lounged on his high seat, hat pulled down over his eyes, a cigarette drooping in the corner of his mouth. He was waiting until we called for him.

Turk, Vincent, Barstow and I, a couple of paces between us, lined up at the front steps in a file. We moved around the house like the second hand on a watch. The first time past the back steps I looked down at the place where Billy Bennett had sprawled, blown away and dead. Each circle it widened. It looped. Fifty yards from the house, then a hundred and a second hundred.

Deep in a patch of land that hadn't been cleared for planting. Clumps of brush. Barstow, in the line on my right, spotted it first. He stopped and squatted. His hand swept like a blade under one side of a low, wide clump. He brought out a scattering of clay. Vincent leaned past him, grabbed that piece of brush, and pulled it out of the ground. It came out easily and showed fresh clay where the roots had been.

I tested the place with my weight. The earth gave. It felt spongy. Turk, off at a distance, saw my nod and put two fingers to his mouth. He blew an eardrum breaker. At the other side of the house, the digger engine coughed and started up. It crawled around the house and bug-walked its way toward us.

It was a forty-five minute flight from Atlanta to Nashville. Vincent had rented a car. It was an hour-and-a-half drive to Smythtown. It had been handled the usual way. No Bureau, state or F.B.I., trusted the local law. All Turk knew was that we were on the way. The digger, on a flatbed truck, was waiting for us at a parking lot a block or so from the police station. Vincent had requisitioned it from the highway department. The operator had seemed happy to see us. It was, I think, double time for Sunday work. What Turk thought about it, he'd kept to himself.

We could have done it with shovels. Three feet down and I saw the foot and the leg up to the knee. I waved the digger away. I got a shovel and crabbed my way down the side of the hole. It wasn't so much digging as scraping. Five minutes of work and the outline was there.

I held up the shovel handle. Turk grabbed it and pulled me out. By that time, Barstow was back from Turk's car. He toed the edge of the hole and took a dozen or so photos with a Polaroid.

I leaned against the digger and got my breath. Eyes closed, I could see her open mouth packed with dirt.

"That's Ellen Webster."

I threw the shovel down and walked away. I sat in the back of the rented car and waited. The rest of the shit belonged to them.

❖ ❖ ❖

Turk's house looked like a used sporting goods store. Fishing tackle and rifles and shotguns all about the house. There was even a fishing creel under the sink in the bathroom. I'd stubbed a toe on it after I'd finished a shower.

I dressed again, except for my shoes and socks. I walked barefooted into the living room and found Turk and the two T.B.I. men spaced around the cluttered room, waiting for me.

"Tell us about it," Vincent said.

I brushed off my feet and put on one sock. "About what?" I'd explained most of the reasoning behind the trip before Vincent and Barstow agreed to it.

"The why of it?"

I tugged on the other sock. "I wish the fuck I knew."

Turk passed me a glass and an open bottle of J.W. Dant. "But you took us straight to the body."

A sip of the Dant. "That was an educated guess. The pieces seemed to fit."

"Make another guess," Vincent said.

"This is a bastard one," I said. "I think somebody doesn't want the Parker murder opened up again."

"That simple?"

"Or it's that complex." I slipped on my shoes and buckled them. "Your people have any guess about when it happened to Ellen Webster?"

"Hard to say." Vincent pointed at the bottle, and I passed it to him. "We'll know more later, but the early guess is sometime Thursday."

I had a question for Turk. "Emma Terry back in town yet?"

"No sign of her."

"Somebody better find her soon." I stood up and looked around for my jacket. "Or she'll be in a hole too."

The young cop without the acne drove me to Nashville so I could catch an 11:23 to Atlanta. I found out his name was Fergusson McCrea. It was a fairly long drive to make with somebody you didn't know. To pass the time, we talked sports. He was a Reds fan, and I said that was like pulling for God and Jesus and the Virgin Mary.

The Falcons didn't interest him, and he didn't understand hockey. Hunting was his real sport. He had his own dogs. He talked about one blue tick hound he had like he was married to it.

Hunting led us to Turk Edwards. I said I thought that Turk did a bit of hunting now and then.

"Lord, don't he," Fergusson said. "I think he'd live out of doors if he didn't need a phone."

"Must be hard getting the time," I said. "The job he's got and all."

"Naw. Most of the time the place takes care of itself. Of course, there are times like the festival when he's got to be there." He laughed and slapped the steering wheel with the palm of his hand. "And tricky? Let me tell you about it. He's got Mayor Brett in his pocket. Like this festival. He goes over to the mayor and says … that was the first of the month … that he wasn't hired to handle all those tourists. He makes such a case out of it that the mayor gives him a week off, to rest up, before the festival begins."

"He take it?"

"Just got back Monday," Fergusson said.

"Get anything?"

"Not a smell," Fergusson said. "Boy, was he hot."

We made the Nashville airport with time to spare. There was no problem with booking a seat. There were only five passengers on the flight.

Darkness below. Some lights now and then.

In a few days, after the T.B.I. released it, the body of Ellen Webster would be making the same trip.

CHAPTER FOURTEEN

leaned against the doorbell for a minute or two before I saw the first light go on near the back of the house. By my watch it was three-ten a.m. There was a warm, damp breeze blowing, and I could almost smell the green part of spring coming in. It was June 2nd, and it wouldn't be long before Atlanta was a city of green leaves and lawns and parks full of kids and dogs and birds.

Hump stayed in the car. I could see the wig-wag of the coal on his cigarette. From the low position of the glow, I was sure he'd scrunched down in the seat. He didn't like being parked in front of a house in Ansley this dark part of the morning.

Another minute or two and the overhead light in the living room went on. I could hear the footsteps coming closer to the door, and then the porch light flared at me. I blinked into the light and realized that I hadn't, even with the time I'd had during the flight and the drive in from Hartsfield Airport, decided how I was going to say it. There just wasn't any easy way.

Nathan Webster cracked the door a couple of inches, saw that it was me, and swung the door wide. "Mr. Hardman, it must be important if…"

I broke in on him. I didn't feel like doing the southern social thing, the apologies and such. "Can I come in?"

He stepped aside and let me past. He closed the door and stood looking at me. In the closed-in room, I thought I could smell something like the scent of some old perfume, one with verbena or jasmine in it

"Maybe we'd better sit down," I said.

Docile, child-like with sleep, he sat on the sofa. I took the soft armchair near that end of the sofa. I cleared my throat and I'd about decided how to start it when I got a rush of that same perfume. I looked over the back of the chair and saw the woman. She was tall and stately and slim, in her mid-fifties, and her hair was that silver-blue color that older women seem to like. The woman had the same eyes and the same thin mouth that Nathan had, and I knew, without the introduction, that this was Nathan's mother.

"Nathan, what is it this time of night?"

Her voice had the same accent, the same inflections. I stood up and faced her.

"Mother, this is Mr. James Hardman. He's been doing some work for me." Then to me: "Mother's just arrived from Charlottesville for a visit."

Mrs. Webster drew her robe together with thin, chalk-white hands. "You appear to work strange hours, Mr. Hardman."

"At times it's not the kind of work I like," I said.

"I don't understand what kind of work you could be doing for Nathan." As she spoke, she moved across the living room. Her walk was erect, an effortless glide. She'd learned posture and walking in a good school.

I waited until she was seated next to Nathan. Then I could sit down too.

"Is it about Ellen?"

"Mother ..." He wanted to protest, but he really couldn't.

I said that it was. Briefly, with lean words and no coloring, I told them about finding Ellen Webster's body in Smythtown. I said that they'd probably be hearing from the Tennessee police in the morning, and I hadn't wanted them to get the word that way, without any warning.

I stood up. "I won't stay any longer."

Mrs. Webster thanked me. I was watching his face. At the end of it, his face looked like a picture puzzle with several pieces missing. I said good night and went to the door. Before I opened the door, I looked back at them. Mrs. Webster had an arm around his shoulders, and she'd pressed his head down into her flat breasts.

The last image I had, before I pulled the door open and stepped outside, was of her face. It showed a fierce and angry tenderness.

I carried that look with me down the dark streets, the car window down and the wind blowing in my face. It was still there over a drink at my house before Hump left to drive home. All right, her face said, I may have won by default, but I won.

There was a note on my pillow. It was from Marcy. *When you get through (tired of?) playing Philip Marlowe, call me.*

It was my morning coffee, but it was two in the afternoon before I made it and carried the cup up the slope to the terrace garden. Chin on the wall, eyes on the ground level, I could see tiny cracks in the earth, places where the dirt was being pushed up and away. The garden was coming up after all. It was the only good news of the week.

Art and Hump arrived about the same time. They came around the side of the house together in a mock argument about Henry Aaron. Art took the redneck position of some of the Atlanta fans that Henry couldn't hit his weight, and Hump was pretending that he took the statement seriously and he told Art that Henry had slimmed down since he'd moved to Milwaukee.

Art leaned a hip against the wall and said, "I tried to call you but you didn't answer."

"It's too damned much trouble," I said.

Art raised an eyebrow at Hump. "Your man's in a bad mood today."

"Getting old," Hump said. "Not only can't cut the mustard but can't find the jar."

"Too much Tennessee last week," I said.

"I talked to Vincent, the guy from T.B.I.," Art said. "He's impressed with you."

"Sure," I said.

"Hell, you might get a job offer."

"That'll get about as far as the references."

"Well, one thing tells you something. They let you out of Tennessee." He nodded at Hump. "Hump was too smart to make the trip."

I blinked at him.

"They had you right there where they didn't need extradition. Could have tossed your butt in the slammer."

That was true.

"I'll write you a glowing reference." Art tipped his head at Hump. "Hump will, too."

"That's right, boss."

"We might need a job." I took a last look at the garden. All it needed now was a light rain or two. I started for the back steps.

"This favor finished?"

"Looks like it, Art."

"Done in Tennessee?"

"I think so."

They followed me into the kitchen. I added fresh tap water to the kettle and lit the gas burner. "The bad news is that I can't draw unemployment."

Art got down a cup and placed it next to mine. "Ellen Webster's death, that might have put a stopper on both cases, the conspiracy to murder here and the Parker murder in Tennessee. That seem odd to you?"

"The whole damned affair gets odder and odder." I rinsed my cup and added instant coffee to mine and to Art's. Hump shook his head and got a Bud from the refrigerator. "You're up early again, Art. Your hours get changed?"

"I woke up with this feeling."

"Tell me about it."

Hump turned a chair and straddled it, his elbows on the back arch of it. He looked sleepy but he was alert, listening.

"I said to myself, now Jim might think he's done with this job. But I know that ugly old mind of his, the way it works. He's been setting himself problems and trying to forget about them and waiting to see what floats up."

"That's about half right." The kettle began its rumble boil. I made the coffee and put a cup in front of Art. "I've been trying to empty it out, but it won't go away. Hell, I never was in this. By the time Hump and I had our first solid lead, the one that took us to Smythtown, Ellen Webster was about one step away from being dead. For all I know, she might have been dead. Well, I found her in a clay hole and it ought to be done."

"But you're not satisfied?"

"Not by half," I said.

"And you're still chasing it?"

"Like a kitten after its tail."

"Let's do an *if*," Hump said. "If we were still in it, what would be the next move?"

"Easy." I had a taste of the coffee and realized that I hadn't put in any sugar. "No, deciding would be easy. Doing it would be hard." I used Art's spoon and stirred in a couple of pinches of sugar.

"I like this hair-splitting," Art said.

"It builds the suspense," Hump said.

"The only tie we've got is Emma Terry, also known as … any damned name she wants to call herself. The way I see it, she drove the VW to Atlanta. That was part of the cover-up, a kind of misdirection play. If anybody was looking for Ellen Webster the road starts here, not in Smythtown."

Art nodded. "I heard you sell that to the T.B.I. men."

"It's one chance in a hundred that Emma Terry is still in Atlanta. If she's got any sense. It's too hot back in Tennessee."

"Maybe," Art said. "And that's a big maybe."

"The question is, what does an unemployed, has-been, fat and forty ex-madam do with herself in Atlanta?"

"That sounds like a Waylon Jennings song title," Hump said. "Could she trick?"

"For the guys at the old folks home."

The chair back creaked under Hump's weight as he stood up. "Let me make a phone call."

It was fifteen minutes and Lord knows how many phone calls before Hump returned. He dropped his empty in the trash can and nodded. "They call it the Rodeo Circuit. That means bare-backed riders for all occasions. Atlanta's the hub. Trains, planes and buses leaving every few days in all directions. New girls for old, a straight trade."

"What area?"

"The way I hear it, it's South Carolina, Georgia, Florida and Tennessee. Met this girl once who was just back from Knoxville. She stopped over a few days before she headed for Jacksonville."

"Vice might know something," Art said.

"Just talked to this old hooker with bad feet." He looked at me. "I said we'd drop off fifty on her later today."

"Fine."

"The word she sold me is that it's a big organization, and that most of the recruiting and the booking goes through a dummy talent agency way out Peachtree almost to Buckhead."

"It got a name?"

"Models and Talent, Inc."

I found the phone book under the bed, blew the worst of the dust cotton candy off it and carried it into the kitchen. I found the listing, ran a crease under it with a fingernail and turned the book toward Art. He copied down the address and said, "I'll check this with John Hedge over at Vice."

After he left for the bedroom, I grinned at Hump. "I didn't know you knew any old hookers."

"They're the only nice ones," he said. "The greed's burned out of them."

"I'm a respectable businessman." Arnold Keppler waved a pudgy hand toward the two framed certificates on the wall next to the door. One was the business' membership in the Chamber of Commerce. The other noted that his agency was a member in good standing of the Federation of Atlanta Businessmen.

We were in the inner office. A mousy girl with a body like a four-by-four, no lumps, no ridges and no bulges, had wanted to stop us at the reception desk. John Hedge, a dapper little man who looked like he ought to be wearing elevator shoes, flipped his ID at her and told her it was police business. That got us past the desk at a fast walk.

"And this is a legitimate business," Keppler said with a dramatic flair. He slapped a palm on the center of his desk. "And, perhaps I shouldn't say this, my taxes pay your salary."

"Some of what I hear is not good," John Hedge said. He took his time looking at his note book. The hesitation might not have been for affect. The lighting was so dim he might have had trouble reading his notes.

Arnold Keppler fitted the seedy grandeur of the office. The furniture gave me the feeling that it had been repossessed from the offices of some con man who'd tried to set himself up as an Atlanta film producer. Now, his point made, Keppler sat back in his high-backed leather chair. He blinked at John Hedge. While he'd been standing, I'd seen the badges of the Atlanta businessman, the white belt and the white shoes. His face was going to jowls and his dark brown hair looked like it might be a wig. I was waiting for a look at his neck so I could be sure about the wig.

"You know a Linda Ross, a Betty Carpenter, a Jenny Burk?"

"Should I?" Keppler said.

"They say you tried to recruit them," Hedge said.

"For what?"

"As hookers," Hedge said. "To go out on your Rodeo Circuit."

I saw Keppler's mouth tighten. I edged toward Hump, who was thumbing through a model and actor's book put out by one of the legit agencies. Hump lifted his head and winked at me.

"That's absurd," Keppler said. He'd been hit hard. I could hear the wind leaking out of him.

"I've got statements from them," Hedge said. He looked over his shoulder at Art.

Art stepped close to the desk, until his legs were braced against the front edge of it. "We're looking for a woman who might be in Atlanta. She goes by the name of Emma Terry, Betty Franklin, Betsy Franks and any number of other names."

They hadn't hit him hard enough. I could feel the control coming back. "What do you want this girl for?"

"She hasn't been a girl for a long time," Art said. "She's forty or a bit better than that."

"Then, of course, she is not the kind of model I'd use," Keppler said.

"She's more the management type," Art said. "A madam."

"A foreign lady?"

Hump hooted at him. At the sound, Keppler turned in his chair and looked at the two of us. "Are you police officers, also?"

"I'm Jim Hardman."

Hump closed the book with a smack and gave him a little bow. "Hump Evans."

I watched him write our names on a pad.

Art pushed at him. "Do you know this woman?"

Keppler didn't answer. He pushed the button on his intercom and said, "Miss Tarver, would you place a call to Richard Wyler of Didler, Bacon and Wyler? You'll find it listed under law firms." He flipped the intercom button and lifted a bland, assured face toward John Hedge. "I assume if you had a warrant that you would have served it by now."

"That's right," Hedge said.

"Can I also assume that if you had more proof than the word of these three women, you'd have brought a warrant with you?"

John Hedge did a slow, easy turn and looked at Art. The look said, what the hell did you get me into, anyway?

The intercom buzzed. Keppler leaned forward. "Yes, Miss Tarver?"

"Mr. Wyler is in conference. His secretary wants to know if he can return your call in twenty minutes."

"Tell his secretary to tell Mr. Wyler that the police are in my office right now, making wild accusations about my business."

"Yes, Mr. Keppler."

Arnold Keppler leaned back in his red leather chair. His face said, it's your move now.

Hedge closed his note book. "That may not be a wise move. We're only asking questions now. Next time, it might not be questions. Think about this, Keppler." He looked up at the ceiling and closed his eyes. "How'd you like it if every woman who came out of your office was stopped and questioned? How'd you like a patrol car parked out there on the curb all day?" He lowered his head and opened his eyes. "That's not a threat. It's a possibility." He smiled. "I saw it in the movies once."

Keppler had started it with the call to his lawyer, and maybe he wanted to stop it now, but he didn't know how to back away. "Is that all?"

"All for now," Hedge said. "You think about it."

Art and John Hedge left together. I heard Art say something to the secretary in the outer office. Hump was watching me. He wanted to know if I wanted him to do one of his wild black man acts. I shook my head at him and tilted my head toward the door. He went out and, as an after-thought, pulled the door closed behind him.

Keppler stared at the pad where he'd written our names. "Yes, Mr. Hardman?"

"Just between us?"

"I don't know exactly what that means," he said.

"Some advice. Good advice. This is a rank business we're talking about. Two or three killings we know about, and the woman, Emma Terry, is right in the middle of it. You protect her and all this other crap is going to fall all over you. Crap that has nothing to do with you." I leaned over the desk, turned the pad that had my name written on it, and wrote down my phone number in inch high numbers. "You'd better believe me, Keppler. This flesh business is something we don't care about. Couldn't care less. So you play this right and you won't be whipsawed."

He'd listened. He tapped the pad with my phone number on it. "What's this for?"

"Have her call me."

On the way through the outer office I heard him on the intercom. "Miss Tarver, cancel that call to Richard Wyler."

Out on the street Hump leaned against the building front and stared at a couple of spring girls who'd taken off their sweaters and discovered they hadn't been wearing bras all winter. I stopped next to him and said, "That's third string."

"Coach your own team," he said.

I laughed at him and drifted down the street to where Art and John Hedge were. Art, patient and waiting his time, was getting it blown out at him. Hedge said, "... doing their dumbass work for them and ..."

"Come on, Johnny," Art said. "The Rodeo Circuit talk melted his glue. The rest of it was bluff."

"Easy for you to feel that way. Somebody's going to ask me why I walked right into that office and laid out all I knew ... without really knowing anything. And that call to his lawyer is going to bump all the way down to me in no time at all."

I leaned in. Hedge did a two-step away and braced his butt against the hood of his car. I ought to be used to it by now, the reactions I get from cops. Not wanting to be too close to me and not sure how they're supposed to act around me. "Keppler cancelled the call to the lawyer. I'll book you twenty that you won't hear from it."

"On my pay?" But you could feel him stop sweating.

"Two to one?"

"Tell me something," Hedge said. "I don't know how it is out in the real world. What did we get done up there?"

"We passed the word," I said. "And we spoke with a forked tongue. One fork said we wanted to talk to Emma Terry. The other fork said we thought it was not nice for him to be nice to her right now."

"All that?"

"All that."

Art clapped Hedge on the shoulder. "Jim learned it in an Arco book."

"There'll be a fugitive warrant on the Terry woman in a day or two," Art said. He was driving us from Buckhead to my place. We were going against the afternoon traffic heading away from the center of town. "That would put the F.B.I. in it."

"We can't wait for that."

Art took a left past White Columns to get us out of the traffic. "That wasn't a nice thing we did to Hedge."

"A favor for a favor. He didn't get hurt."

Not much more talk. Each of us pulling inward, drawing in tight. Down long, tree-lined streets, past the Ansley Country Club and the golf course. Lulled by all that green.

Art pulled up in front of my house. From the car I could look at the lawn and see the bare spots, patches where it needed re-seeding. Fat chance. Only if the neighbors came by and did it one afternoon while I was out.

Art said he'd try to put some people on checking the hotels. On short notice, Emma Terry might have to use one of the names she'd used in the past. Until she had time to establish a new identity.

"You?" Art said as I got out.

"If we punched the right button I ought to be getting a phone call."

"You, Hump?"

"He's with me," I said.

I left Hump with the phone and drove to Peeples Liquor Store. I loaded two cases of Bud into the back seat and walked around the wine section until I found a bottle of a Macon Blanc that had a label I could read. Fred Peeples had the tab figured and I counted it out while he bagged the wine. Along with the change, he passed me a sealed envelope.

"Didn't take a week," he said.

I didn't bother to count it. The count was always right. The bills would add up to $950. After I got home, I'd have to do some figuring and decide how much I ought to return to Nathan Webster.

On the way home, I looped over to Ponce de Leon and bought three pounds of shrimp at the fish market.

I reached home just in time to get a call from Marcy.

The Philip Marlowe note, according to her, was a joke. I laughed politely and invited her to supper.

※ ※ ※

The phone rang a bit after ten. We'd had supper and we were watching the Braves game that was being televised from Montreal. It was too early in the spring, and it looked like it might snow before they got in five innings.

Marcy was nearest the bedroom. She started for the phone. I waved her away and closed the door to shut out the TV sound.

"You know who this is?"

The voice didn't mean anything, but I made my guess. "Emma."

"You want to talk to me?"

"I want to see you," I said.

"You must think I'm dumb."

"You pick the spot," I said.

"What's in it for me?"

"Maybe a break for you when it goes to trial."

"No way." I could hear the breathy laughter. "If it goes to trial, it'll go without me."

"Heading out?"

"I'm not welcome here anymore. That's thanks to you."

"I want to see you before you leave."

"I'm not going to walk into anything," she said.

"There's no warrant on you yet that I know of."

"And that's supposed to be a reason why I should see you?"

"You've seen the paper?"

"I saw it."

"There'll be a fugitive warrant on you in the next day or two," I said.

"You were there?"

"With a shovel in my hand."

"I didn't have anything to do with that. I just drove the car to Atlanta."

"But you knew what was going to happen?"

"I guessed. No, I just thought it was going to be rough on her."

"And better her than you, right, Emma?"

"Yes."

"Pick a place for a meet. I'll come alone."

"No, I've seen you with Turk. I don't trust you."

"Turk's in Tennessee. What's Turk got to do with not wanting to ... ?"

"You dumb fuckhead, don't you know anything?"

She slammed the receiver down. I sat on the edge of the bed and listened to the dead sound on the line.

CHAPTER FIFTEEN

Marcy left at daybreak. I remember the warm bed scent of her and a kiss with the taste of toothpaste in it. And then I rolled over and slept until nine.

I dressed in jeans and a T-shirt. After I put on the coffee water, I walked down the front steps and looked for the *Constitution*. The paper boy's arm was going. The paper was lodged far back in a pyracantha bush. That was the expected. The unexpected was parked on the curb.

It was a new black Continental.

I couldn't see the driver. I stood on the steps and stared at the Continental until the driver got out. Even with bleary eyes I could recognize him by his bulk. The driver, now rounding the back of the Continental, was Carter Williams.

He stopped in the center of the lawn. "I want to see you, Mr. Hardman."

I searched the tone. He didn't seem angry. I worked the rubber band from the rolled paper and waved him up the stairs. "I'm about to make some coffee."

While I made the coffee, he sat at the kitchen table. His head craned this way and that. I could feel him reading me by the furnishings and the way the house was kept. Compared to his house on Fortune Road, it was a slum. Still, it wasn't as bad as usual. After supper the night before, Marcy had given the kitchen a cleaning, and Hump had put out the trash before the beer bottles and cans became a hazard.

"You want to see me about Ellen Webster?" I slid a cup across the table toward him.

"I understand you were there when they found her."

I pushed the milk carton and the sugar dish back toward the center of the table. "I did some of the digging."

"How?"

"How was she killed? Shotgun."

"Bad?"

"I've never seen a pretty dead body," I said. "Not after the undertaker finished either."

"I decided I ought to talk to you."

"Your lawyer, Markman, know about this?"

"No." He lifted the cup and his hand shook. "He wouldn't like it. He checked on you."

"I heard."

Coffee slopped over the rim of his cup, and the harder he tried to control the shaking, the worse it got. I watched the coffee rain down upon the table. "He told me about the favors, the ones you do now and then."

"It's a living."

"You're working for Nathan now?"

"Until Sunday," I said. "Now, I don't know."

"Could I hire you?"

I tore three or four paper towels from the roll and spread them over the spilled coffee. "It would depend on what you want. And I'd need some straight talk from you."

"It won't go beyond this room?"

"I can't promise that. If you're involved in some crime…"

"I'm not, unless sleeping with a woman is a crime."

"So, you're finally going to level?"

He sipped at what was left in his cup. "I thought about it most of the night. I've been parked outside for most of an hour. I guess it's time."

It began about three months before. That would put it at the end of February. He'd never really paid much attention to Ellen Webster. Oh, he'd noticed that she was an attractive woman and all that. Any man would. The end of February, he'd realized that she was obviously putting herself in his way. Every time he turned around, she'd be there. It was flattering, it did wonders for his ego, and that was when he took her to lunch for the first time.

It was after the second lunch, when she'd fought back tears during the telling about her problems with her husband, that they'd made love the first time. She'd still been disturbed, and he'd taken her into his office after they returned to the Foundation. She'd broken down completely, and one moment he'd been comforting her and the next moment they were making love on the rug. It had been world-shaking, amazing, the best and the most exciting. Touching her had been like touching flame and not being burned.

There'd been other lunches, and there'd been evenings when she could find some excuse to leave home and meet him. Those meetings had been arranged with care. She'd drive to the parking lot at Ansley Mall, not far from her home, and she'd be met there by Billy Ray Price. Price would drive her to the apartment.

"Often?"

"Two times a week," Williams said.

"And Billy Ray knew about the affair?"

"He had to, but, like I said, he was more a friend than an employee."

"Where did you meet?"

"Fortune Road was out of the question. Billy Ray rented an apartment on North Highland in his name."

"And afterwards Billy Ray would drive her back to the parking lot?"

"That's right."

"Both of you have cars on those nights?"

He looked puzzled.

"After he dropped her, did he have to drive back to the apartment to pick you up?"

"No, he used his own car."

"So, there's no way of knowing how much time Billy Ray really spent with Ellen Webster? He could have driven her straight to the parking lot, or he could have spent an hour with her or even two hours?"

I'd planted the seed. The question we'd asked him that time at his house hadn't reached him. He'd been so sure that Billy Ray was the perfect employee and good friend, it had slipped right past him. And, of course, he must have believed in Ellen.

"How serious were you two?"

"I don't know."

"Any talk about marriage?"

"You always do," he said. "Even if it's just to save the woman's feelings."

"Any talk about her getting a divorce?"

"Some. Now and then. But I'd told her that I wasn't sure I could risk having my name involved in a messy divorce case."

I left him for a few seconds and found part of a pack of smokes near the TV set. I lit my first of the day. "And when you told her that she said ... ?"

"She said she thought she could convince Nathan to give her a divorce without letting him suspect there was another man involved."

"It's straight up time," I said. "You have anything to do with trying to hire the professional?"

"No."

"You didn't know what Billy Ray was doing?"

"How could I?"

"You didn't go to the motel that night and try to convince Billy Ray to drop the hunt?"

"I didn't. And I didn't kill him and beat you up if that is what the question means."

I lit the burner under the kettle. I kept my back to him. I didn't know for sure that he was telling the truth. Not the one hundred percent truth. Still, it had the right sound to it.

"You said something about hiring me?"

"Yes." He placed a hand over the top of his cup when I brought the kettle to the table.

"What am I supposed to do for you?"

I watched him while I mixed myself another cup of coffee. He hesitated. The words wouldn't roll out. I knew then that it wasn't the standard job I'd be getting. It wasn't the find-out-who-really-did-it crap.

"I want to be sure that my name is kept out of this ... no matter what else happens."

"The way I see it, you're out of it," I said.

"Huh?"

"If you didn't try to hire the killer, if you didn't kill Billy Ray ..."

"I didn't. I swear I didn't."

"Then you're home free." And got screwed and blowed at no expense, at no cost to you.

"I feel better." He brought out his checkbook.

I shook my head at him. "Let's see how it works out. It works out for you, if you're left out, you send me a check for five hundred."

He replaced the checkbook. I saw him to the door. He said the usual things about feeling better now that he'd told somebody about it. I nodded like I believed him.

After I closed the door behind him, I cleaned off the kitchen table and had that second cup of coffee and read the *Constitution*. I'd reached the sports page before the timing hit me.

Three months. Yes, that was Cora Abse for you. The Parker case was breaking open one state over. She looked inside herself and saw that she needed the protection that big money could give her. She needed to change her name and her feathers one more time. If she worked it right, if she married Carter Williams, it would not be hard to manipulate him. There were so many other places to hide. New York and San Francisco and even Europe. Who'd look for Cora Abse on Park Avenue or Nob Hill or at the Ritz Hotel or the south of France? Nobody.

So she'd put it to him. All that wonderful screwing, and he could have it if he kept her happy.

Moving on time. Cora Abse knew all about that.

My father died in 1952, while I was in Korea.

Back in the 1920's and 1930's, he'd worked in the textile mills in North Carolina. It had been a time when the unions were moving in and organizing, and there'd been the bloody strikes and the busted heads and the broken arms and legs.

I was born in 1931, and Mama didn't like what was going on so she'd pressured him. She'd said, "Mr. Clem, this is not a place to bring up a child." You see, she'd had great hopes for me. I'd be the first one in the family to graduate from college and I'd go on to be a great lawyer or a doctor.

The pressure worked. We leapfrogged South Carolina and ended up in Carsonville, Georgia. Mama had a sister living there. In time, Daddy worked his way up from mail carrier on the rural backroads to postmaster.

He never forgot the language of the textile workers. He'd use a word or a phrase, and we'd give him a puzzled look and he'd laugh. It's been a long time, and I've forgotten most of those words and phrases. Only one of them stays with me now. I guess I remember it because it was the summer I was fourteen and I was just getting interested in women. A lady that went to the same church with Mama and Daddy, a lady they respected a lot, suddenly, with no warning, up and ran away with the Watkin's man. I don't remember the man, but I remember those trucks.

The Watkin's trucks covered the backwoods in the south, selling coffee and spices and needles and thread and a hundred other things farm women needed.

The day we heard what had happened, we were on the porch after a heavy supper. Daddy waited until Mama went in the house to refill his iced tea glass, and he said to me, "I always thought Mrs. Jennings had a cotton heart." He was a kind man, a man with a massive understanding. He didn't mean anything harsh.

It turned out, back in the textile days, that was the way men talked about the women who worked there. If they could be led this way and that, if they could be talked into walking too far in the woods on a dark night, they'd wink and say, "A cotton heart on that one."

Cora Abse-EIlen Carver-Ellen Webster? No, not really a cotton heart the way those men meant it.

Too deadly for that. If she had a heart it was as hard as the shell on the seed in the center of the bole.

It was cocktail hour at 590 West, the bar on the top of Stouffer's Inn on West Peachtree. It was early in the week and slow. As the week went on, it would crowd and fill. As the week moved on toward Friday.

I'd spent the rest of the morning, after seeing Carter Williams, waiting to see if Art would call. He hadn't. I guess nothing had come of the look-see at the hotel registrations. At four, Bill Barstow, the T.B.I. man, called. He'd flown in alone to talk to the Atlanta police. They locked in tight on Emma Terry ever since they'd bought my theory that she'd had driven Ellen Webster's car to Atlanta and that had taken us to the grave on Rock Farm. Like me, they'd arrived at the conclusion that the woman was still in Atlanta.

I agreed to meet him for a drink. Now we were seated at a window table on the front side of the bar. Our table overlooked the Crawford Long hospital complex and beyond that the northwest section of town with its old houses and all those trees greening over.

"No way to pressure Keppler at the talent agency again?"

I said I didn't see how we could do it. He'd done about as much as we'd asked him to. He'd cut her loose, unprotected I thought, and he'd probably told her to call me. That was as far as I thought he'd go. He wasn't about to turn her over to us, not with what she knew about his operation. If anything, he'd told her to call me, but that she'd damn well better keep her distance.

"I'm not sure your way was the best one," Barstow said.

"It's all risk," I said. I sipped my gin and tonic and looked down at the street. "You just come in from Smythtown?"

He said he had. I watched him having trouble with the stalk of celery that came with his Bloody Mary. He didn't want it and it was too long to fit into the ash tray. He solved the problem by eating off a couple of inches before he dropped it in with the cigarette butts.

"How's Turk?"

He laughed. "That bastard. You know what he did? He went to the mayor and complained that he didn't like the way Vincent and I came waltzing into his territory without so much as a hello of warning. He raised hell and more hell, and he decided that he needed a week off so he could calm his nerves."

"He just got back from a ..." I laughed along with Barstow.

"That's what the mayor said. But Turk said it was either that or they could have his badge and the shitty job."

"And he got it?"

"Starting yesterday. Monday."

"That's balls," I said.

"If I'd tried that," Barstow said, "I'd be on the street looking for a job."

We agreed that things were run funny in Tennessee. A puffy woman with fat fingers sat down at the piano and began playing rock songs scaled down for a two-step, and we had another drink and I said I had to leave.

Like a lot of cops I knew, Barstow was dull as cooked carrot tops. About all he knew was his work.

I was relieved that Art was wrong. There was no talk about offering me a job.

CHAPTER SIXTEEN

Hump's dusty Buick was parked in the shady part of the lot to the right of his apartment building. The front door, usually locked, was propped open, letting in some fresh air to blow away the stale fall and winter smells.

Hump came to the door wearing a pair of cut-off jeans and a tie shirt with a collar so frayed that it looked fringed. "You didn't bring any fried chicken with you, did you?"

"Hungry?"

He motioned me in and left the door open. "This being unemployed hurts."

"The shorts?"

"So-so," he said.

I got out my money fold and spread it. I worked three twenties out of the bottom. "That hold you? I can get more from the house."

"This ought to do me for a day or two."

I sat down and looked at the zipper scar that ran up the side of his right knee. There was one on his left knee, too, but it was only about half as long. "That's two-sixty of the five hundred. Your half of the thousand from Webster. Soon as I can see him again, I'll see if he wants some of it back. I thought I'd give him a couple of days before I talked to him."

"I trust your math," he said.

"Want some supper?"

"I could use a rib sandwich."

I grinned at him. "You're not going to get me in that neighborhood again." One night, when he had me beered out, he took me to a black place far out Auburn Avenue. He'd enjoyed the hell out of himself. I'd thought I was going to have to donate a couple of my ribs just to get out of the place.

"A honk cafe's all right with me."

"Gene and Gabe's?"

I called Marcy and caught her before she checked out of the office for the day. She said Gene and Gabe's was fine with her, that she'd meet us in the lounge in half an hour or so.

Hump returned from the kitchen and tossed an envelope to me. "Amuse yourself with this while I get dressed."

The envelope was postmarked Nashville. There wasn't a return address. From the postmark I could see that it had been mailed late the day before.

"Who do you know in Nashville?"

"Read the letter."

He went into the bedroom. I sat in an easy chair and slipped the letter out of the torn end of the envelope. The letter was written in smeared ballpoint pen. It began *Dear Old Buddy.*

I flipped the single page over and read the signature. *Turk.*

"How'd he know where to reach you?"

"Cops have ways, I guess."

Dear Old Buddy:

Here I am getting drunk in Nashville. It's the vacation I've been promising myself for about ten years. Usually I spend time off hunting. I'm writing this at a booth at the Orchid Lounge, and there is a girl a couple of tables over that makes me think this might end up as bird hunting. She's got red hair about down to her ass and it is some ass.

Guess that is about all. If I can work it out, I am still going to make it to Atlanta this fall. That'll be for the first Falcon game, whenever that is. You buy the tickets, and I'll bring the booze. It ain't that I miss the game. I just like to watch those dumbasses killing each other while I'm sitting up there in the cool with a drink in my fist.

Say hello to your fat friend, Jim.

I folded the letter and stuffed it back in the envelope. I dropped it on the coffee table and went and leaned in the doorway. "Sounds like he's having fun."

"Odd thing about that letter," he said.

"Yeah?"

"There doesn't seem to be much reason for writing it. That strike you?"

"Drink getting to him," I said. "You two really that close at Cleveland?"

"No more than I was to five or six other guys."

I shook out a smoke and packed it against the door frame. "How long's he been out of football?"

He counted it back while he flipped his way through the jacket section of his closet. He selected a dark blue double-breasted and slipped it on. "I quit in 1968. Turk got retired the year before that. That would be 1967."

"Got retired?" I lit the smoke.

"Turk was like a lot of the guys. Don't know when to quit. Want to hang around another year or two. They haven't socked much away and don't seem to worry about it until it happens. In 1967 he must have been near thirty-four. That's not old, but it's not young either. Pre-season that year he was getting beat often. Coach took him aside and tried to talk him into retiring. He wouldn't hear it. Did his best to catch on with another team, but the word was out. Too slow, too old."

"Rough," I said.

"Funny that we're talking about this. It makes me remember. That dude owes me a hundred. I loaned it to him the day he left camp. He said he was heading back to Tennessee and needed some plane fare."

"Remind him the next time he's in town."

"That won't do any good," Hump said. "He's had eight years to forget about it."

Marcy tailed me home from Gene and Gabe's. Hump left us during the coffee and cognac. He said something about a foxy lady he wanted to drop by and see.

The wind had the feel of rain in it. Marcy changed into a pair of jeans and a shirt of mine, and we sat on the terrace wall and watched the stars get clouded over. When we couldn't see the stars at all, I figured that we only had minutes before the rain.

"You're quiet tonight, Jim."

I felt a drop of rain hit my nose. A small one. Still some time. "It's this booze-rotted head of mine. It's like something is trying to push through and I keep yelling that it's a wrong number."

"Trying too hard?" She leaned against me and I put an arm around her shoulders.

The rain began feather soft. I stood up and steadied her when she slid off the edge of the wall. It got stronger, heavier, as we walked down the slope to the house.

After midnight. The clock ticked. I could hear it played off against Marcy's bubbling snore. Sifting it, sorting it, walking around it to see it from all sides.

It wasn't over yet.

At four a.m. exactly, the phone rang. It was Emma Terry.

CHAPTER SEVENTEEN

"Why'd you change your mind?" I hooked my shoes with a couple of fingers on my free hand and pulled them toward the bed. The socks were stuffed inside. I lifted the left one and shook it and tried to put it on one-handed.

"You could say it's economics," she said, "I'm tapped out, and I figure you owe me."

"How much?"

"Five hundred'll get me located somewhere else."

The sock went on twisted. I tugged at it until I got the heel straight. "You must think the banks open early in the big city."

"How much you got on you?"

"Two-fifty," I said. "But it's not free. You've got to talk to me."

"I'll tell you what you want to know."

I tried the right sock. I got it over my toes, but a nail caught and I had to start over. "If you'll wait until later in the day, I can have the five bills."

"No way," she said.

"All right. One hour from now, and this better not be a box like the last one."

"It's not. I swear it's not. And you're coming?"

"I'll be there."

She broke the connection. I straightened both socks and dialed Hump's number.

"Where?" Hump asked after he got his mind working.

"The bandstand in Piedmont Park at five a.m."

"That's a death trip," Hump said. "The entrances are chained off from midnight until about seven in the morning. You'll have to park outside and walk it. You'll be a slow-moving target."

I said I knew that.

"Meet you at the clubhouse in twenty-five."

I dressed in the dim light from the bathroom. The last stop was the shoebox in the back part of the shelf in the closet. I took the box into the bathroom. The .38 P.P. was on top of the cash. I stuffed it in my waistband and separated five fifties from the money stack. I didn't think I'd need the cash. It wasn't, I thought, going to be that kind of deal. A hundred to one it was a set-up, but I prepared for that slim chance that it was straight.

Marcy awoke when I closed the closet door. She sat up and rubbed her eyes. "What time is it?"

"Something after four."

"Are you late dating on me, Jim?"

"It's that damned Webster thing."

"Be careful."

I leaned over and kissed her. Her morning mouth wasn't as bad as some I'd tasted. She relaxed and turned her head into the pillow. After all this time, I guess she was used to it.

I passed the Piedmont Park Golf Course clubhouse. There was no sign of Hump's Buick. I checked my watch. Still ten minutes before he was due. I continued down 10th past the Charles Allen Drive entrance to the Park. The chain was up. I took it slow. I seemed to be the only car on the road that time of morning. At Piedmont I took the right turn. Four blocks down I passed another entrance. That one chained also. Speeding up and on my right the Piedmont Driving Club whipping by. One more entrance. That one chained too. One way so I couldn't turn and head back the way I'd come. Faster and I reached Monroe and turned right. Blowing straight down Monroe like it was a raceway.

I reached 10th and found Hump's Buick parked in the Thompson Air Conditioning lot beside the clubhouse. I pulled in next to him. He got out and waited.

"I hope you've got some bright idea, Jim."

"I think I threw out all the dumb ones."

We walked down 10th past the clubhouse. To the left, across the street, there was the Grady High football field. Just beyond the clubhouse were the steps that led down to the greens. I touched Hump's elbow and we turned and walked down the flight and reached the practice putting green.

I angled toward the water treatment unit. A fetid smell blew from that direction. A concrete drainage ditch sliced across the course. We crossed the footbridge, and we were on the greens once more. It was an odd course. If I remembered right, the golfers had to play at least one shot across the road that handled a lot of the traffic that passed through the park.

We reached the embankment that bordered the road. We followed the road, staying below it, until I was certain we were level with the made-made lake and the bandstand. "About right?"

"I think so."

I climbed the embankment and dug my feet in to steady myself. I fell forward on my elbows. Across the road the lake was dark, and there were no lights at the bandstand. Hump crawled the bank on my right. Shoulder-to-shoulder, we stared across the road.

"How long before first light?"

"An hour, a bit more," he said. "So that's the move?"

"I ain't about to cross that road. The way I see it, if she really needs the cash she'll wait. If she doesn't it's a set-up, and I've missed my chance to get dead."

I settled in for the damp wait. Next to me, Hump shivered.

❧ ❧ ❧

At six, the sky was lighter. I could see the gray outline of the bandstand near the lake. No movement that I could see. At six-fifteen, I said to hell with it and stood up. It was a slipping and sliding climb to the road. Hump followed me, and I turned and waved him twenty yards away from me.

My legs were shaky. I was having trouble getting a deep breath. I didn't like it much. I got the .38 from my waistband and carried it down by my leg.

"Looks clear," Hump said.

"Somebody at the bandstand," I said.

Fifty yards. Half of that. "Emma?"

I could see the shape of the heavy woman. She was seated on the top bandstand step, back braced against a side post, head down on her knees.

"Emma."

On my right Hump ducked and sprinted for the bandstand. He stopped and looked down at her. One close look, and he whirled toward me. "Jim."

I reached past him and touched the side of her face. Cold. I squatted and peered at her from the side. Her neck was at a strange angle. Probably broken.

Hump stepped back and began to circle the bandstand. There was a woman's pocketbook on the step below the body. I picked it up and opened the clasp. Before I could dig about in it Hump said, "Here, Jim." I snapped the clasp and, still carrying the purse, followed him. He pointed at a place where the damp ground had been stomped down into a sort of half-circle.

"One stood here," Hump said. He continued his loop around the back of the bandstand. "And here." He toed the edge of another spot that showed the shoe prints and the signs of long and nervous waiting.

"Two of them," I said.

"Gave up on you."

"Must have." That was twice. How dumb did they think I was? I said, "No reason to stay here."

We reached the embankment before I realized that I was still carrying Emma Terry's purse. I stopped, turned back, and then decided it was too much trouble. Hump went over the embankment like a skier and I followed him. Back the way we came.

I'd tossed the purse into the front seat and said, "My place?" before I heard the first siren. It sounded like it was coming up 10th from Peachtree. That siren was joined by another one that I placed somewhere near Ponce de Leon and Charles Allen.

I backed and turned in the lot so I could reach Monroe without turning onto 10th. Hump was a bumper behind me.

The box hadn't worked, so somebody had tried a frame.

I didn't know what to do with the purse. I dropped it on the kitchen table and patted Marcy on the butt while Hump was in the bathroom washing up. She turned, started to say something and saw the pocketbook.

"What's that?"

"Some ex-hooker's purse."

"You take up mugging, Jim?"

"I might as well. Nothing else is working." I got two more cups from the shelf. Marcy poured in the water and I spooned in instant coffee. I put the cups on the table and went into the bathroom and shooed Hump out.

After I washed up, I returned to the kitchen and found that Marcy had dumped the purse on the table top. "I've always wondered," she said, "what a hooker carried that other women didn't."

I sipped my coffee and watched her. Lipstick, Rolaids, a compact, half a roll of candy mints, some used wads of Kleenex, a checkbook on the First National Bank of Smythtown, a plastic wheel of birth control pills.

"Nothing unusual so far," I said.

A silver hairclip. A small purse bottle of perfume. Marcy spritzed a mist on the back of her hand and sniffed it. "Awful."

A pack and a half of Newports. A Bic lighter. A few hairpins. A handful of change. A Tennessee driver's license in the name of Emma Terry.

"Any folding money?"

Marcy unzipped the compartment inside and brought out a thick fold of bills. I took them and ruffled them and dropped the wad in the center of the table. More than four hundred. She'd been lying. She hadn't been tapped out.

"What else?"

"Nothing," she said.

"That by your elbow?"

"This?" She tossed me a book of matches.

"Jokers Wild?" I looked at Hump.

"A bar in the back of the Peachtree Manor."

Marcy returned all of it to the purse except for the money and the book of matches. "That wasn't as educational as I thought it would be." She placed her cup in the sink.

"Some days are that way."

She kissed me and left for her apartment. She'd have to change clothes and it would be a push to make work on time.

A lighter and matches? Maybe and maybe not.

It was a day for long shots. I carried my cup into the bedroom and looked up the Peachtree Manor Hotel. I dialed the number and asked my first question. It missed by a mile. There wasn't a Emma Terry registered.

Hump walked in and stood at the foot of the bed.

The desk clerk said, "Is there anything else, sir?"

What the hell. Why not? "Is there a Mr. Edwards staying there?" I saw the surprise on Hump's face.

Silence on the other end of the line, and then the clerk said, "Yes, there is a Mr. Edwin Edwards with us."

I put my hand over the phone. "First name Edwin?"

Hump nodded.

I thanked the clerk and hung up.

"You've got to be kidding," Hump said. "That man's the law."

"And it's not football season yet, and he's supposed to be in Nashville."

I made two calls. The first one got Art out of bed. The second one was to the T.B.I. man, Barstow, at Stouffer's Inn.

"That dude," Hump said with a kind of finality, "never was as smart as he thought he was."

CHAPTER EIGHTEEN

I t was a few minutes after ten. We were parked in the lot across the street from the Peachtree Manor Hotel. I was in the back seat with Hump, and Barstow was in the front passenger seat. It was Art's car, an unmarked police one, and he was across the street in the hotel. He'd been there about ten minutes.

"Tell me a funny story, Hardman." Barstow put his arm on the seat back and turned to face me.

"It's got a lot of guesses in it," I said.

"Go ahead, I like your guesses."

"That man in Huntsville prison ..."

"Martin," Barstow said.

"Martin said if he named one of the men involved in the Parker robbery-murder it would surprise you people. What's more of a surprise than a police chief being involved in that about four years before he became a police chief?"

"That might qualify," he said.

"Once upon a time there was this football player, and he got cut by the Cleveland Browns in the fall of 1967. He really had the shorts, so short he borrowed at least one hundred from a defensive end who didn't know at the time it was his last year, too. Maybe he worked for a time in Tennessee. Maybe he fell right in with some tough guys and did some jobs. One job they did was in Gaptown, where they killed and robbed a retired dentist. Word always gets around about this doctor or that dentist who's got it socked away. Maybe Parker did. Anyway, after that job this retired football player probably stayed in Nashville for a time. And I think he met Cora Abse there. The Abse broad was set up fine. Her man, Lippmann, had gone to the slammer and he'd left her set up well. All the money she needed and a car and an apartment. All she was supposed to do for that was keep her knees together until Lippmann got out. And her mouth closed, too. The only problem was that Cora liked men, and Turk was a man. I don't know how long this lasted, but it was long enough for Turk to do some drunken bragging about his part in the Parker killing. It might have been his way of proving he was the equal of the man she was supposed to be waiting for."

Art came down the steps from the lobby of the Peachtree Manor. He stopped under the tunnel-like awning that ran out as far as the sidewalk. He looked both ways and then he jaywalked across Peachtree to the car. He slid behind the wheel. "Turk Edwards and some young guy named Ed Beuller have been registered here since late Monday night."

That fitted. Turk and Ed had driven from Smythtown to Nashville in the late afternoon Monday. On the way through town, he'd mailed the letter to Hump. It was a letter that was supposed to say, here I am in case anybody wonders where I am in the next few days.

"Not in?" Barstow said.

"Checking out at noon. I think they're having breakfast somewhere right now." Art opened his note pad. "It's a blue 1975 Montego, probably rented." He read off the tag numbers. He placed the open pad on his leg. "I guess we wait."

"Go on with the fairy tale," Barstow said.

"I think the word got to Lippmann in prison. Cora was living it up too well. You know how this works. He sends somebody around to see her, and that somebody offers to break both her arms and legs and probably does put a lump or two on her head. By then the ex-football player is gone. He can't protect her, and she is mad with Lippmann, and after the shoplifting bust she decides to break Lippmann's balls for good. From the ex-football player, she knows enough details about the Parker murder. It's ranker than anything Lippmann's pulled. And she puts that on him and his friends."

"Where's Turk all this time?"

I grinned at Barstow. "You beginning to believe this? He's probably in Smythtown. He's found out that crime pays, but the hours are bad and he's beginning to get known in town. Famous jock and all that. He's two or three years away from being named police chief. Imagine his surprise when Cora lays the Parker murder on Lippmann and that bunch. Not that he minded at all, but you can bet he is in touch with Cora Abse right after the trial. Maybe there's still a bit of an itch. And maybe he suggests she move to Atlanta."

"And they keep in touch?"

"I'd say so. I think they set it up that way. The first year he's police chief, he sends her a circular on the bluegrass festival. Maybe a note on it. She tells her husband she's got a high school reunion and shows up in Smythtown. And you can bet they had a real reunion. And everything is going well. He's very, very sure of her."

"And three months ago that guy, Martin, opens his mouth and the case is about to re-open," Art said.

"Turk's in a sweat. Who's going to take Martin's word against his? But there's the main witness, and he's got to be sure about her. He sends her the festival circular. No answer from her. He sends her a couple more. What he doesn't know is that she's sweating, too. And she's planning to make a move of her own. Turk gets so worried he takes some time off... to go hunting he says... and he shows up in Atlanta. He probably sees her and she reassures him, but Turk is not convinced. He follows her around for a day or two, and he sees her with Price. And then he follows Price around, and I think he gets close enough to know what's going on. I suspect he got a smell of it."

While I'd been talking, I watched a tall, stoop-shouldered man come out of the parking lot stall and stand looking at us. Now he started a long-legged, angry stride toward the car. He leaned in Art's window and said, "If you're going to park in this lot you'll have to come by the office and get a timed ticket. Otherwise, how'll I know what to charge you?"

Art showed him the ID. "Police business," he said, "and now get the fuck away from here."

We watched him walk back to the stall, a bit more stoop-shouldered. He went in the stall and closed the door behind him.

"My guess is that he followed Price and saw Price go to the motel where he'd reserved the room for the meeting with me. He barged in and he and Price had some words. Price didn't make the right answers, and Turk used a blackjack on him. A few times too many. And then, dumb me, I knocked on the door and walked in."

"You have a talent for it," Hump said.

"And the nose to prove it," I said. "Cora or Ellen or whatever freaked out. Price was supposed to free her of Nathan Webster and he hadn't, and the police were asking questions. She did the only thing she knew to do. She bugged out for Smythtown. It was intended as a retreat, a time when she was going to decide her next move. But Turk had had enough. He and the sharecropper, one or both of them, did her in and buried her on Rock Farm."

"And then you showed up and started asking questions?" Art waved two fingers at me, and I passed him a smoke.

"He doesn't panic. He's still thinking well. He revises his plan. He knows that if I can trace Ellen Webster to Smythtown other people can. So he plans to have Emma Terry drive the VW back to Atlanta. But first he has Emma set me up for Bennett and his shotgun. That doesn't work, and he's in a bind. Turk and that kid, Ed, could have covered for Bennett. The other young cop, McCrea, knew right away the description fitted Bennett. So Turk had to follow through. He's going to go through the motions. He might even arrest Bennett until I leave town. He tries his best to warn Bennett. He yells something about this being police business. The young cop, McCrea, spoils it again. He yells from the side of the house that he's got Bennett on the hip. Bennett thinks he's been sold out and makes his run ... right into Ed's shotgun."

"It's got holes," Barstow said.

"Sew them up," I said. "You're the cop."

Art leaned forward and stubbed his cigarette out "Heads up."

I followed his gaze and saw the blue Montego turn onto 6th street and then swing sharply to hit the ramp and head into the parking lot. The Montego passed the parking lot booth and turned left and pulled into a space in the same file with us, but five or six cars over to the right.

Art said, "All of you stay put. You're out of it."

"Careful," I said.

Art hit the door handle and stepped out. His coat swung open, unbuttoned. Iron on his hip and ready.

As soon as the door closed behind him, Hump said, "I don't like this. It's two to one."

"Art's got surprise on his side," I said. "They don't know who he is."

"You've never seen Turk in action."

I watched Art. He stepped over the low concrete bumper that separated the parking lot from the sidewalk. He swung right, headed for the Montego, but you wouldn't know it from the way he moved. It was slow and easy and he even took time to give the eye to some early morning hooker out for a free walk.

Turk locked the door on the driver's side. He looked like money today. He was wearing a pre-faded and splotched denim suit that must have cost a lot more than it was worth. On the other side of the Montego, Ed Beuller slammed his door and backed away.

It looked good, very good. Art was two cars away. Count to a slow ten and it would be over.

The first brick fell out. Ed Beuller, the young cop with the acne, waved at Turk and headed for the parking lot booth. Going for the timed ticket, I thought.

Still possible. Art could brace Turk and when Beuller returned with the ticket the collar would fit him too.

Beuller was halfway between the Montego and the parking lot stall when the stoop-shouldered man ran out of the booth. He was looking past Beuller, and I knew that the second brick was about to fall. I said, "God damn," and hit the door handle and stepped out of the car. Hump didn't quite understand, but he followed me.

I heard only the last part of what the parking lot attendant yelled. "… don't care if you are a cop you've got to pay just like …"

Beuller understood it first. He took off at a run. I made one step in that direction, but Hump passed me at a run. Beuller reached the 6th street sidewalk and sprinted to the right. Hump cut across the lot, going at a long-legged trot. Even with a bad leg, Hump could outrun me on the best day I ever saw.

I turned back to Art. As soon as the attendant shouted, he made his jump for the space between the Montego and the Ford station wagon on this side of it. His coat was tucked back, hand on the butt of his pistol. He said, "Turk, don't move."

I didn't believe it. It happened and I saw it and I still didn't believe it. Turk had been looking over the roof of the Montego, trying to figure what was going on. When Art called to him, he began a slow turn. It was so slow that there didn't seem to be any danger in it. Then it changed. It was so fast it was a blur. One step and he was close to Art. He hit Art two or three times, about as fast as I'd seen anybody hit. Art fell back and sprawled on the sidewalk.

I'd thought it was done, and now it wasn't. I pushed off and ran for the sidewalk. I was slow and flatfooted. On the way past Art, I looked down. He wasn't out, but he was dazed and the trickle of blood had started out of his right nostril. As soon as he was sure Art was down, Turk turned and fumbled with the keys. He got the car door open and he was half in and half out. His back was to me, and he didn't see me. I took a run at the door and slammed all my weight against it. It hit him and hurt him, and I tried to pin him there. I kept hoping Barstow would show up. Turk recovered, and he was strong. He turned and pushed against the door. I fell back, my heel hit the concrete bumper and I landed on my rump. I was like that when Turk came after me. I leaned forward, trying to get to my feet. His knee hit me in the face, and I did a double fat roll and landed on top of Art. He grunted and in some kind of reflex, he pushed me away. Maybe he thought I was Turk. I tried to get to my feet, but Turk was right on me. He caught me and lifted me and threw me against the front of the Ford station wagon. He threw a right that hit me heart-high, and I thought my heart had stopped for good. I was rumptight against the station wagon grill. He kept punching me. Body and then face, body and then face. I wanted to fall, but he'd lean in and give me a push that straightened me up and another right would come out of nowhere. My face didn't have any feeling anymore, and I knew that if he kept hitting me the bone would be mush. I leaned forward and when he stepped in to push me upright, I saw my chance and butted him. My forehead hit him across the bridge of his nose.

As soon as I saw the pain on his face, I almost said I was sorry. That was how dazed I was. I had a flash of a time when the school bully was picking on me and I'd hit him, and I'd known right away that it was going to be hard on me. And it had been.

Turk was mad, really mad. His hands dropped from my chest, and I pulled and twisted away. It surprised him, and the right he was throwing at my belly missed me and struck the station wagon grill solidly, head on. Even above our breathing I could hear the bones go. The right hand wasn't any good anymore.

Turk's face showed it. He knew and I knew, and he tried to back away. I kicked out at his feet, and he tripped and fell on his back. I jumped on top of him. The right hand came up and stopped about six inches from my face. He knew better. That hand dropped, and he threw his left into my ribs. After all that pain, I hardly felt it. I drew my right back and hit him in the mouth. I kept hitting him. I didn't know how long it went on. I was still swinging when Art and Barstow caught me under the arms and pulled me off him.

Turk looked like raw meat. I knew I looked the same way.

Art put an arm around me and held me up. I looked across the parking lot. Hump headed toward us. He had Beuller by the back of his neck, half pushing, half dragging him.

I spat out a mouthful of blood. It landed on Turk's new denim suit pants.

Hump and Art dropped by later in the day. I was in my bed. Both hands were bandaged, and they'd taken fifteen stitches on my right cheek and eight on the underside of my chin. Hump cracked the seal on the bottle of J&B he'd brought with him, and Art got glasses from the kitchen.

"You ought to be in the hospital," Art said.

"You don't look too good either," I said.

And we talked the rest of it.

Turk wasn't seeing anybody but doctors at the moment. Ed Beuller, his boy, thought up something new to tell every time Art told him that Hump wanted to see him. Ed had seen enough of Hump.

It went this way. Turk saw it was falling apart. It scared him how easy it was when we'd gone to Rock Farm and found the body of Ellen Webster. He'd been smart enough to know that Emma Terry was the last tie. But she was in Atlanta somewhere, and I was looking for her. He knew that. And maybe he'd have never found her if I hadn't mixed in and put the pressure on her.

Emma decided she could use this to her advantage. As soon as she heard from Keppler at the talent agency, she called Turk in Smythtown. He'd been about to leave for Atlanta to look for her. That was luck. He'd told her to call me and play hard to get so I'd be set up.

On Tuesday they'd met at the Jokers Wild behind the Peachtree Manor Hotel and put together the plan. They were going to box me one last time. They didn't want me to have the time to do any planning. That was the reason for the four a.m. call. Emma Terry, no longer useful and a danger to Turk, had been dead even before Hump and I arrived at the Park.

After two drinks, Hump and Art were ready to leave.

"What about the Parker murder?"

"That's still in the air. With Ed Beuller's testimony, we've got Turk for Emma Terry's murder. The rest of it will depend on Turk, when he's up to talking."

Art carried the glasses into the kitchen. Hump leaned over me. "You had your mean up out there today."

"He hurt me. Right up to where I'd decided I couldn't be hurt anymore on this side of dead."

"I've been there," Hump said.

Marcy took one look at the way I moved and said I'd be in bed for a week if she had her way.

During the night I woke up sweating. I was soaked and the sheets were, too. Marcy heard me grunting and trying to get to my feet. She changed me to fresh p.j.'s and put a cold cloth on my face. I guess I was feverish.

I said, without knowing that it was coming, "You know, Marcy, you've got a cotton heart, too."

"What does that mean?"

"That you're a soft, soft woman."

"That's nice, Jim." A cool hand rubbed my chest.

Before I dropped off again, I told myself, all right, so that's not the way the textile workers my father knew meant it. But words mean what you want them to mean. And I meant soft, soft woman.

The scent of her perfume was soft and delicate around me when I dropped into the dark pit.

I tried to call Nathan Webster a few times in the next week. He didn't return my calls, and I thought that meant he didn't want to talk to me and I forgot about it. I split what was left of the Webster money with Hump.

In late October, when the new telephone books were delivered, just on a hunch I looked for Nathan Webster in the white pages. He wasn't listed anymore.

I knew then he'd left town. If I had one guess, I'd say that he is probably in Charlottesville. And that he grows cold and gray in the shadow of his mother.

HARDMAN'S WORLD

By Robert J. Randisi

M any careers have been influenced by Chandler, Hammett, Ross Macdonald, Spillane, mine included. But 12 books by an under-appreciated writer had a drastic effect on my work, and my love of the P.I. genre.

In the 70's, I was trying to get published and writing P.I. fiction, a genre all of the editors I met were telling me was dead. Robert B. Parker's *The Godwulf Manuscript* came out in 1974. It was the first book to feature Spenser and Hawk. The critics loved it. So did the readers. But that same year, I discovered Ralph Dennis and Hardman, and my attitude about the genre changed.

Okay, I admit the covers attracted my attention first. It was the 70's, when vigilantes were booming, and Popular Library decided to publish Ralph Dennis' private eye novels. But they packaged the books to look like a men's adventure series, along the lines of *The Executioner, The Penetrator* and *The Destroyer* books published by Pinnacle. It was too bad. The series lasted 12 books, but the men's adventure audience probably did not take to it, and the private eye audience likely never found it. It was great work sabotaged by the publisher.

But even at age 23, I was the kind of reader who looked beyond covers. And I was constantly on the lookout for new private eyes. So what I found was 12 excellent books in the P.I. genre.

Jim Hardman was decidedly un-men's adventure-like. He was an ex-cop, unlicensed, middle-aged and overweight private eye. His sidekick, Hump Evans, was a black retired NFL football player. As a fan—or "nut"—for the genre I was immediately pulled in to Hardman's world. Dennis' style was lightning quick and not hampered by unnecessary bogged-down narrative or run-on description. The characters were real, people you ether knew or wanted to know. And to me the works showed no obvious influence by the classics. Yes, this was definitely Hardman's world. And it all worked.

And Ralph Dennis proved to me—the budding P.I. author—that you didn't have to be totally influenced by those classics. Here was something new that I could point to as an influence because the series was fresh and hip as hell.

Seeing Paul Newman play Harper when I was 15, and discovering Ross Macdonald, put me on the path to private eye writing. Ralph Dennis and Jim Hardman convinced me I was on the right road, and there were new ways to travel it.

On his Thrilling Detective Website, Kevin Burton Smith described Hardman perfectly as "one of the great lost eyes."

Well, here he is, found again. And 12 books was way too few.

Robert J. Randisi is the author of more than 600 novels (no, that's not a typo!) and the founder of the Private Eye Writers of America. He is returning to the PI genre with his Auggie Velez/Nashville books *The Honky Tonk Big Hoss Boogie* and *The Last Sweet Song of Hammer Dylan*.

ABOUT THE AUTHOR

Ralph Dennis isn't a household name ... but he should be. He is widely considered among crime writers as a master of the genre, denied the recognition he deserved because his twelve *Hardman* books, which are beloved and highly sought-after collectables now, were poorly packaged in the 1970s by Popular Library as cheap men's action-adventure paperbacks with numbered titles.

Even so, some top critics saw past the cheesy covers and noticed that he was producing work as good as John D. MacDonald, Raymond Chandler, Chester Himes, Dashiell Hammett, and Ross MacDonald.

The *New York Times* praised the *Hardman* novels for "expert writing, plotting, and an unusual degree of sensitivity. Dennis has mastered the genre and supplied top entertainment." The *Philadelphia Daily News* proclaimed *Hardman* "the best series around, but they've got such terrible covers ..."

Unfortunately, Popular Library didn't take the hint and continued to present the series like hack work, dooming the novels to a short shelf-life and obscurity ... except among generations of crime writers, like novelist Joe R. Lansdale (the *Hap & Leonard* series) and screenwriter Shane Black (the *Lethal Weapon* movies), who've kept Dennis' legacy alive through word-of-mouth and by acknowledging his influence on their stellar work.

Ralph Dennis wrote three other novels that were published outside of the *Hardman* series but he wasn't able to reach the wide audience, or gain the critical acclaim, that he deserved during his lifetime.

He was born in 1931 in Sumter, South Carolina, and received a masters degree from University of North Carolina, where he later taught film and television writing after serving a stint in the Navy. At the time of his death in 1988, he was working at a bookstore in Atlanta and had a file cabinet full of unpublished novels.

Brash Books is releasing the entire *Hardman* series, his three other published novels, and his long-lost manuscripts.

www.ingramcontent.com/pod-product-compliance
Lightning Source LLC
Chambersburg PA
CBHW021231020726
47498CB00008B/2801